MUSTANG SPRING

MUSTANG SPRING

Stories & Poems
by
Deanna Dickinson McCall

Published by The Frontier Project Inc.

Inquiries: The Frontier Project Inc.
PO Box 7160, Pueblo West CO 81007
www.frontierprojectinc.com

Designed by Emily Kitching & Steve Bell,
Eclectic Horseman Communications, Inc.
www.eclectic-horseman.com

ISBN: 978-0-9853425-3-1

CONTENTS

For Dave and Rusty,

who gave me the gift of time to write.

FOREWORD

We still run a cow outfit.
Most of the old ways still fit
In a changing land and time
Taught by the Old Ones of mine.

From "The Old Ones,"
by Deanna Dickinson McCall

Five generations of ranching course through Deanna McCall's veins, through her life, through her writing. She has become one of the "wise ones." As is the responsibility of tradition, she carries the wisdom forward through her absorbing poems and beckoning stories.

Like life, she's complicated. She can offer up a poem as spare as a swept bunkhouse, followed by a story complex in plot, character and suspense. Or, the reverse, with variations. Her tales are unfailingly moving and insightful.

Her wisdom is hard-earned. Her stories are not about the "romance of Western life." Characters know heat and hurt, cold and loss, danger, heartbreak and toil. But, like the writer, they don't know "can't." Perseverance is required for survival. When there is humor, it is wry, ironic, a way of coping with ever-present challenges of ranching life.

She removes any mythical gloss of that life. Like the effects of a desert's endless blowing sand, what remains has a high polish. Her poems and stories shine, their underlying themes reflecting a firmly rooted sense of purpose and a fiercely protective embrace of an honorable way of life — one worth all struggle.

Deanna McCall is not the last of a dying breed, though the life she lives and writes about is in constant peril from what some call "progress." She, like those before her, helps take a stand against such threats through her storytelling and in the way she lives her own life. The precious legacy is in more-than-capable hands.

Read Deanna McCall's work and enter her world. Be a witness to admirable endurance, character and art. Relish the writing. Be fortunate to receive the wisdom.

Margo Metegrano
Center for Western & Cowboy Poetry

THE OLD ONES

I was raised by Texans, and am part of the first generation on my Granny's side, since the 1840s, not to be born there. They taught me strength, tenacity, and most of what I know about cattle and horses. They were truly men to ride the river with.

Before most life began to stir
The tinkling of bit and spur
Would make music and carry on
In the early light before dawn.

Voices floated on the soft air
Like an old melody hung there
Played and sung by slow Texas drawls
Held in by the steep canyon walls.

In my troubled dream
They lived again, it seemed.
The Old Ones readied to ride
Grass ropes coiled at their sides.
Split reins gathered in gloved hands
They rode proudly for their brand.

On strong horses they rode away
Into the foothill mist of day.
I cried in vain for them to wait
As they went out the corral gate.

They both turned and I saw their eyes
And knew this was the last good-bye.
Dad and Granddaddy riding away
With me pleading for them to stay.

Feeling my own heart pounding,
I heard their voices sounding
And felt the crash in my chest
As their mere words pierced my breast.

I woke aching with deep regret
Wringing wet with my own stale sweat
For the Old Ones had spoken true
And now I knew what I must do.

The Old Ones were gone again
The last of my clan and kin.
Proud men of horses and stock
They were my shield and my rock.

The message in the dream was clear
To gather strength and show no fear.
The Old Ones had taught me so well
And in my heart and soul would dwell.

We still run a cow outfit.
Most of the old ways still fit
In a changing land and time
Taught by the Old Ones of mine.

Before most life begins to stir
The tinkling of bit and spur
Still makes music and carries on
In the early light before dawn.

MUSTANG SPRING

The sky was Nevada blue on an August day in 1986 when the haying machines shut down in the mid-afternoon on the high desert ranch. The sweet herbal smell of meadow hay drifted up to the old ranch house that sat on the bench above the meadows. A young woman stood leaning with her arms crossed, lost in her thoughts, staring out the antique screen door at the lush meadows below. She was preoccupied with her thoughts of water, cattle, hay and a baby.

"You check Hillside Spring yet? It wasn't producing much last time I was there," her tired husband asked as he grabbed the gallon jar of tea. "You'll have to take your dad's truck, and walk up the hill. The four-wheel-drive isn't working right."

"Not yet, James, I was waiting for the baby to wake up. I'll go now while you all are resting and I won't have to pack him up the hill," Sue replied evenly. It was a hastily made decision she would never regret. She grabbed the long-sleeve shirt she wore for protection against the high desert sun as she went out the door.

When the rich meadows were ripe for harvesting, Sue took

over most of the responsibility of keeping track of the cattle and their water supplies so that James could concentrate on the vital hay crop to put their cattle through the winter. Their baby accompanied her almost everywhere, in the truck, in the fields, on the vast range, wherever her work took her. He'd been horseback at two weeks of age, snuggled against his mother in his pack, lulled to sleep by the horse's hoof fall.

Sue drove down the dusty road, following the curve until the road bisected the grassy bottomlands and crossed the valley. A lone mustang was grazing. Pushing a strand of sun-bleached hair back under her ballcap, she scanned the area, puzzled that she saw only one horse, as they usually traveled in bands and were a familiar sight. This horse must have been kicked out for some reason. The studs had been fighting lately over bands of mares, she mused, so he'd probably lost the battle of being the dominant male. He'd find some mares of his own. With over two hundred head on the ranch at any given time, he would form his own band soon enough.

Pulling to the side of the dirt road, she parked the truck and climbed out into the dry August heat. The ranch dogs jumped out, landing joyfully in the alkaline dust. They loved to go with her, and ran ahead, smelling for jackrabbits to chase as she began the climb up the rock-strewn hill where the hidden spring lay near the top.

Halfway up the trail, Sue felt an odd urge to look behind her. She was startled to see the horse was now at the pickup. He threw his shaggy head up suddenly and reared, looking straight at her. Sue felt a chill run through her and rubbed her arms despite the warmth of the dry desert air. The horse's front feet landed, causing a puff of white dust before he began to run toward her up the rocky hill. She began waving her arms and yelling, intent on letting him know she was a human, and thinking to turn him away. Her movements seemed to only spur him on.

She began to hurry toward the spring, where a few sparse juniper trees grew, stopping occasionally to turn around and yell again at the horse, trying to frighten him away. She watched the muscles bunching, saw his necking stretching out, felt his burst of speed as cold terror raced through her.

Focusing on the small group of scraggly trees, her knees lifting higher and higher, Sue raced for her life. Chest heaving, she climbed into the first stubby juniper just as the horse came lunging up. The dogs sensed her fear and began barking, then attacked the horse as he came skidding up to the tree where she was breathlessly perched. She scrambled to get higher and heard a sickening thud followed by a yelp. She saw one dog propelled through the air land in a small gully below her.

"Back, back!" she commanded, fearing for the dogs, knowing full well they would give their lives for her. As she turned her head away from the dog lying in the rocks, hooves struck the tree's trunk below her bent knees, skinning long strings of juniper bark. She saw the ranch headquarters below in the distance and prayed for someone to come outside and hear the dogs.

Sue fervently searched for somewhere, anywhere, to go when the horse's head came flying up into her face. The horse's graying, scarred face with its ugly, broken, yellow teeth barely registered while his hot, rotten breath struck her like a slap.

"What a hell of a way to die! Thank God I don't have the baby with me!" she thought.

With no sign of anyone in the ranch yard, sad resignation fell over Sue, and she began to picture her death. The dogs attacked the horse again, barking and biting as they charged, renewing her resolve with their tenacity. She took advantage of the distraction to throw herself out of the back of the tree, leaving pieces of her cotton shirt hanging on the branches.

Sue landed on her back in the broken shale that covered the hillside. The fall winded her. She felt the sting and stabs of the rocks, and prayed she hadn't broken any ribs. As the dogs bought her precious time, she struggled to her feet and ran stiffly, crouched over, behind a small bunch of trees, looking for a way to get out of the crazed stud's reach.

To her left, she spotted a trail weaving through a patch

of stunted trees, big sage and greasewood. Glancing back, she decided to risk following it, hoping to remain hidden long enough to give her time to think. Gulping a breath of air, she realized the dogs' barking was less frequent and sounded further off. Peering through the limbs, she saw the dogs were gradually driving the horse back down the hill.

The trail crossed an arroyo a couple of feet deep before meandering across the open hillside. Sue gingerly lowered herself into the arroyo, ignoring her aching and stinging back, and peeked over the rim to see if the horse had spotted her movements. The dogs were still herding him down the hill, and she noted with relief the dog that had been maimed earlier was back with the others, snapping at the horse's heels.

Sue eyed the barren hillside below, then allowed her eyes to cross the valley, her gaze stopping at the ranch and meadows in the distance. She prayed again the family would hear the dogs raising hell and come to see what was happening. Where was her husband's impatience when it was needed? Surely, he would be in a hurry to get back to the fields, unless he gave in to the temptation of the cool house and a nap.

Turning back to look at the mustang, she saw him whirl and stop as he spotted her movement. She flattened herself further, knowing she was in no position for another attack. She felt sweat run into her eyes and could hear her heart thudding as she froze in place, praying the dogs would keep him headed away.

After a few antagonizing moments, she began scooting on her belly down the arroyo. Sue felt the rocks digging into her hands and knees as she crawled on her belly, legs straight out behind her to keep her body as low as possible. Twenty-five feet ahead, the gully became shallower and Sue hoped the stud wouldn't spot her as she quickly wiggled through the area.

Gravel-size rocks were embedding themselves in Sue's hands as she drug her body down the gully. Her back was beginning to spasm from jumping out of the tree. Her shoulders ached and her knees throbbed. Stopping for a second to catch her breath and risk another peek to see what the horse and dogs were doing, she rolled painfully to her side to peer over the rim of the shallow arroyo. The horse was now at the truck, circling it, and marking the area with his manure.

Sue couldn't imagine why the crazy-acting stud was marking the area any more than she could explain any of his other bizarre actions. Stud piles were common enough, to claim an area, but not a vehicle. The dogs sat on their haunches, taking a break, studying the area around the spring for a glimpse of her, and blocking the horse from going back up the hill.

Sue rolled back over, noting the small blood trail she was leaving. She wished the dogs would send the horse further back into the meadow, but didn't dare draw attention to herself by yelling commands to them. With renewed fortitude, she began crawling again. She didn't know how much longer she could keep going or what was going to happen, but knew she couldn't stay where she was. She tried to focus on the family waiting at home.

After another two hundred yards of crawling, Sue stopped again. She was shaking from the tremendous effort of dragging herself through the broken rocks. She closed her eyes and listened for any sound of the dogs or horse. The gully had become very shallow, forcing her to press her body closer yet to the ground. She could barely feel her legs. Numbness had replaced the pain. She tried to keep her hands off the gravelly ground, using her forearms to scoot and pull her aching body. Her hands were bleeding and torn, and her shirt was wearing through, exposing the soft skin underneath.

Painfully raising her shoulders slightly, she turned her head to the right and discovered she had a view of the now much closer truck and meadow. The horse grazed on the edge of the meadow, occasionally throwing his head up to stare toward the spring. Sue sank back to her belly, and prayed the horse would continue to venture further out for better grass. Afraid to move for fear of detection and needing rest and time to gather her thoughts, she laid her head wearily on her aching arm. Tears ran silently down her dusty, scratched face.

After a few minutes, she began crawling again, determined to make it home. At the next low spot, the truck came into clear view. Unfortunately, the dogs spotted her at the same instant, and began running in her direction.

Silently cursing, Sue saw the horse throw up his head at the movement of the dogs. She made her decision in an instant and struggled to her feet, unsure if her legs would support her. She would try to run to the truck, gambling the horse didn't beat her to it.

"Get him up!" she commanded, throwing her aching, tattered arm in the direction of the horse, praying the dogs' attack would give her more time. As she stumbled out of the draw, her legs felt like one of her children's toys, rubbery and bending the wrong ways. Surges of electrifying pain raced through her body as she began a stumbling run toward the truck. Pure adrenaline kept her going as she propelled herself forward across and down the rocky hillside. She would reach the truck or die trying. She continued to yell at the horse, her voice as ragged and raw as her body felt.

The horse whirled again and shook his head as the racing dogs turned back and slid into his space. He tried to turn toward the truck, but the dogs attacked as a pack, two snapping and charging at his front quarters while one hung on his tail and the remaining one nipped at his heels.

Sue gathered herself up and pushed harder, sobbing and yelling as she closed in on the safety of the truck. She wondered if she could jump into the bed and, if she were able to, if it would provide enough protection. Eyeing the battle of dogs and horse, she prayed aloud, between gulps of air, for God to help her. She finally reached the truck and grabbed the bed for support as she made her way to the door.

"Back! Back!" she yelled, and began calling the dogs by their names. The motor roared to life as the dogs came running, tongues almost dragging the ground.

"Jump!" she commanded, and then allowed her weary head to rest against the steering wheel for a moment.

The horse was now circling in the alkali dust, tossing his head toward the truck. The dogs landed with a thud and Sue turned the truck toward home, narrowly missing the enraged, dancing horse. The burning red eyes, the flared nostrils, and the evil emanating from the crazed animal locked into her brain. Her body was shaking so badly she could barely steer. Huge, gulping sobs racked her shaking body as she drove toward home.

Crossing the cattle guard into the ranch yard, she hit the horn several times, and pulled up sideways. When she reached for the door her strength failed her. She laid her head back and tried to draw strength once again from deep inside. The screen door slammed and James came in front of the truck, his walk showing he wasn't fully awake.

"What the hell? You trying to wake the baby?" James said, rubbing his eyes. He looked up at his wife and saw the dusty, bloody, tear-streaked face.

"Help me out. I don't know if I can walk," Sue said quietly before he could go further. He pulled the truck door open and as she turned stiffly to get out, he saw the shredded sleeves and her arms shaking with the effort.

"What the ...?" he began to say and stopped when her knees came into view. Bloody gravel had replaced the denim. He reached for her hand and she shook her head, turning her hands over so he could see the raw flesh.

As he helped Sue in the house, he listened incredulously to the story. Surely, she had exaggerated. It just didn't make sense. Nevertheless, he had never known her to make up tales, and there had to be an explanation for her wounds and shaken state. He decided that, once Sue was settled, he'd see if the horse was still around.

"I'm going down there. I can't have something like that around," he said, after getting her a drink and hearing her story. She was painfully washing the dirt and rock out of her arms and hands.

"I'm going with you," she said, sensing his disbelief.

"The kids can watch the baby while we are gone," she added

as she carefully patted the ragged skin dry. She walked stiffly to the door, and winced as the frayed material at her knees pulled on her abraded skin. The toes of her tennis shoes were almost worn through from the dragging and pushing of her toes. Her husband grabbed a rifle from behind the door and followed her out.

They rounded the curve that gave a view of the bottomland where the horse first appeared. James stopped the truck and grabbed binoculars off the seat.

"I see a horse," he said. "He's behind that bunch of grease-wood, just over that slight rise to your left."

James lowered the glasses and started the truck down an old road that was little more than wagon ruts left from days gone by. They bumped down the crude road and saw the horse throw up his shaggy head, his ragged mane flying. As they came closer to the horse, he began prancing nervously. James slowed the truck and whistled, then made a blowing sound that simulated the sound the studs used. Without hesitation, the horse lowered his head and ran for the truck, tearing the turf as he poured on the speed.

James stepped out of the truck and began to walk toward the oncoming horse. Sue yelled franticly for him to get back.

"Are you nuts? I guarantee that damn horse is!"

As James turned his head to reply, the horse slid toward him, teeth bared and preparing to strike. James caught the movement out of the corner of his eye and dove into the truck as the stud's hooves struck the open door where James had stood a moment before.

James was dumbfounded. He'd never seen a mustang act so aggressively. He jacked a shell into the rifle as he told Sue, "We can't have that here! He'll kill someone! Hell, he may be rabid!"

"Well you sure as hell can't shoot him here, in the middle of the meadow, unless you want to go to prison!" Sue was already shaken to her core emotionally. It was a felony to kill a mustang.

"We're gonna try and get him out of here, up into a canyon where the coyotes and birds will clean him up. I'm also using armor-piercing bullets," James answered. He began driving the truck, honking the horn at the stud, who pranced and swayed, turning back to the truck and taking a few steps sideways. James revved the engine and made the horse run forward. The stud wheeled and, rather than running away, tried to strike the vehicle. After several minutes of this, they neared the first canyon and James got the horse headed into it.

"I don't know what's wrong with him — if he's been kicked in the head, poisoned, or what — but we can't have him around," James said. "What if that was your dad, instead of you? Crap, we can't even ride with something like this here. Next thing will be him coming into the place for our horses. I don't know where he came from, but I know where he's going."

James opened the door and steadied the rifle while Sue closed her eyes and covered her ears. Sue felt the repercussion travel through her body. She hated killing, didn't believe in wasting life. James shared the same principle. However, she also knew it was necessary at times. Her family and their lives came first. The thought of how near she had come to packing the baby up the hill sickened her.

The old graying stud's behavior would remain a mystery. No one ever spotted the carcass. No other horses with his symptoms ever appeared in the valley.

ADVICE

The corrals were full enough to bust
        And we'd all had our share of dust.
But we'd got all the pairs in
        And the separating was about to begin.

Our new son-in-law was working the gate
        Trying hard to discriminate
When an angry one came charging up
        Mad at the hold up!

Hearing the commotion, I rode through the dust
        And shared some advice he could trust.

"Son, don't crowd 'em
        Whatever you do.
When their head's held high
        They'll take the fence, or you.

Better off to just let 'em stand.
        Cool down a bit.
They're not afraid of horse or man.
        Let 'em have their fit.

It's Nature's way to attack or run.
        Fear and anger are part of life.
I know it's not exactly fun
        But, remember, she is your wife."

TOWN BORN

The shiny knobs on the stove all pointed upward in the right direction, the sparkling windows were pulled firmly down against any dirty wind, and the wood floors glowed richly as she took a last long look around. Her green eyes took it all in and yet seemed to stare at something beyond the scrubbed walls surrounding her.

Nothing would ever be the same. When she returned, she would be carrying a baby into this house where she was raised and she would be a mother. Her life as she knew it now would end, and she was stalling.

Jeannie had always been active and physically fit, not really a true tomboy, but there was nothing she didn't do on the ranch, from breaking colts, to driving heavy equipment, to handling all the stock. She'd had stare-downs with angry cows, been bucked off more times than she could remember, and had never had second thoughts about doing anything lots of folks would consider dangerous. But, she had noticed the further the pregnancy came along, so did her maternal instincts. She'd even decided to let the hired hand get in the calving pen when a heifer went berserk, something that was so foreign to her she wondered where on earth the thought had come from.

"Come on Jeannie! We need to go," yelled her husband, as he placed the last of their bags into the pickup. He grinned at the large cloth bag festooned with baby animals; it was his baby's bag! He hoped for a boy, picturing a smiling cherubic face with Jeannie's eyes, but would be happy with a healthy baby. He agreed with the doctor in the small mountain town, that ninety-nine percent of the time it was fine to be born on a ranch seventy-five miles from a hospital, but that one percent could be fatal, and Rob wasn't about to gamble his wife's or baby's life on the odds. The doctor would check Jeannie today and hopefully give them a better idea of when the baby would arrive. The time had come for them to stay in town until the baby came.

Jeannie climbed awkwardly into the cab as Rob came around to shut her door. Her tanned muscular arms lifted her out-of-balance body up into the seat. A glance at the round mound resting on her legs had her wondering once again if she'd ever have the slim waist and firm body ranch life had given her. As her gaze lifted to her chest, she thought of ruined-bagged cows and cringed. Lord, not that!

The long trip into town began with thirty miles of dirt road before they hit the highway. Jeannie swore her back was already aching from just thinking about it.

She was ranch-raised, her family running sheep and cattle, besides registered Quarter Horses. Birth was a natural event, and her delicate yet strong hands had helped with many births, yet she was anxious. She felt no more motherly than the first-calf heifers that ran away from their calves, or the ewes who refused to let their lambs nurse once relieved of the struggle of labor. She prayed the feelings would come, as her mother and aunt had assured her they would.

Rob drove carefully, watching his young wife's face pale under her tan as he hit a bump in the dirt road. He saw her rub her stomach protectively as she closed her eyes, the long lashes lying on her lightly freckled cheeks. She was more beautiful than ever, though she sure was ornery lately. He knew why pregnant mares were called *brood*mares, now. He expected that would change when the baby came — their baby, he thought with another grin.

Houses began to appear at intervals and Rob pulled into the first convenience store he spotted. Being raised in town, he missed the junk food that was absent at the ranch. He hurried into the store, grabbing greasy burritos, corn dogs and soda pop. Breakfast had been a while ago and his belly rumbled at the smell of the hot food. He handed Jeannie a spicy bean burrito and a bottle of pop.

They pulled up to the large yellow house her family had always kept in town, a place to stay when bad weather or business didn't allow a return trip to the ranch. Rob had never appreciated it as much as he did today, and let out a big sigh of relief.

After unloading the suitcases, bags and boxes, and promising himself a nap after their appointment, Rob led Jeannie back out to the truck and they drove to see the elderly doctor at the hospital, who reassured them Jeannie and the baby were doing fine, and that it would be a few days before the birth would occur. Jeannie trusted the kind old gentleman, who had helped her come into the world and had treated her few childhood ailments. He patted her hand and looked over his glasses, winking at her as she left, reiterating the baby would come when it was ready.

Back at the house, Rob climbed the stairs to find a bed in which to rest. He'd been up early, lining out the hands with chores and checking the stock held at the ranch for various reasons. His boots landed with a thud and he stretched out while Jeannie lay down on the couch and tried to get comfortable, her back aching. Rob's snores resonated through the house, challenging the rhythm and racket of a train that began to pass through town.

Jeannie dozed off and was wakened shortly by an urge to go to the bathroom. She rose clumsily from the couch, doubling over while cursing the burritos they'd grabbed for lunch. She waddled to the restroom, gas cramps surging in waves. As she carefully lowered herself to the toilet, water gushed from her, causing the toilet water to back splash.

"Oh, God, was that my water breaking?" she wondered. Another cramp came, and she gritted her teeth.

"Rob, come here, now!" she yelled toward the stairs. Another pain drove through her body and, as she peered between her legs, she saw bloody fluid.

"Rob, damn it, the baby is coming! Get down here!"

Rob woke groggily to Jeannie's yells, once the train had finished rumbling its way out of town, yelling back he would be there in a minute. He groggily grabbed the phone beside the bed, calling the doctor to explain they were on their way to the hospital.

He grabbed the keys and Jeannie's overnight bag and started the truck, then ran back into the house to find Jeannie leaning back in the bathtub, the floor littered with towels, holding a bloody, wet, wrinkled baby between her legs. Reeling in shock, he yelled, "What the hell did you do that for? I was coming! Couldn't you wait?"

Jeannie pushed her hair back off her sweaty face and stared at her outraged husband.

"Like I had a choice!" she replied. As they both stared at each other, they realized how ridiculous the whole thing was and began laughing and crying all at once. Rob knelt down and stroked his wife's cheek and peered at the wrinkled baby while the sound of the ambulance's siren neared. One mile from the hospital and the baby was born in a damn bathtub.

When Jeannie was asked later why she got in the tub, she said it was so the mess would be easier to clean up, and that she had been afraid the baby would drop in the toilet. Both baby and mother were fine when the ambulance pulled up and took them to the hospital. Jeannie's maternal instincts arrived on time and all Jeannie and Rob's babies were born in town, but not all in the hospital.

WHEN THE DAY IS OVER

There are days on a ranch that make you question your sanity...
why you work so hard for so little gain. This poem answers that question for me.

> When the shadows fall on the hills
> and deer tiptoe in to drink
> The porch beckons quietly
> inviting us to rest and simply think.
>
> When the sun starts sliding down
> and the last cow calls her calf
> The night birds start their song
> whispering wings riding a draft.
>
> When the breeze becomes a touch
> and the coolness caresses your cheek
> The surrounding quiet so complete
> you hesitate to even speak.
>
> When the dogs curl at your feet
> and close their weary eyes
> The fatigue mellows in your bones
> as an early moon begins to rise.
>
> When the twilight turns to velvet
> and stars streak across the sky
> The questions and doubts of ranching
> have all been answered why.

BARBED PAIN

The new Dodge pickup, shiny as a candied apple, slowed as it approached the last curve to the ranch headquarters. Virginia felt a tightening of her slim body behind the wheel as the large trees and red barns came into view. The ranch, one of the largest in the state, was where she grew up. The pressure of her college finals that she had just completed was nothing compared to the tension she felt beginning to build. She shook her head, admonishing herself once again that she was twenty-three years old. Definitely time to grow up, she thought sternly.

A herd of grass-fat steers came pouring out a gate into the roadway. Behind the cattle, Virginia spotted her mother on a young bay horse. At almost sixty, Dolly was as trim and petite as her daughter. While her body might've belied her age, her face had the creases and lines of outdoor living.

Virginia pulled in by the largest barn. She closed her tired eyes and took several deep breaths. Calm down, she reiterated to herself silently. She knew and expected Dolly would find something to displease her. Dolly rode the shying colt up as Virginia climbed out of the truck, stiff from tension and driving all day.

"Could have used you this morning," was Dolly's greeting.

Virginia buried her hurt feelings, as she had done for as long as she could remember. She had driven six hundred miles to answer her mother's call that she was needed immediately at the ranch. Dolly and Virginia's father had divorced a few years ago after years of bitter quarreling. Virginia had prayed the relief of the divorce would soften her mother, but it hadn't. Dolly would never be maternal, she realized. Virginia bit back a sudden grin at the thought that if Dolly were one of her beloved cows, she'd be culled for her lack of mothering instincts.

"Your horse is saddled and waiting," Dolly went on. "I never dreamed you'd be here so late. Poor guy has been standing there for hours," she added.

Virginia obediently mounted and followed her mother out of the horse barn. She tried to push aside the fact that her mother hadn't asked about her, the drive, school, any of the questions a normal parent would ask. She was just expected to get on a horse the minute she arrived. The crew of men joining them brought her thoughts back to the ranch. Dolly employed over a dozen full-time men. An older Mexican man rode up beside her and gave her a smile of missing teeth. The remaining teeth reminded Virginia of jagged mountain peaks bathed in golden light.

"Good to have you home," he said as his old brown hand gripped her knee. With his dark eyes searching her face, she felt exposed and vulnerable. Juan had become like a father to her over the years. It was he who had wiped tears from her blue eyes as a child. She shrugged her narrow shoulders and tried to smile back. The smile never reached her eyes.

The riders approached a pen of newly arrived stockers.

"We need to get these processed and out on grass," Dolly commanded. "They've been held up too long, now," she said, sending a pointed look at her daughter as they entered the wire pen.

Virginia felt the stirrings of anger as the ranch hands began building a fire. It was so like Dolly to blame her. It was ridiculous to think her presence there made any difference. What the hell did they do while she was a state away? It was also like her mother to brand the calves in a wire trap, instead of the corrals, complete with a propane setup for branding, on the other side of the barn. Any way to make things more difficult, that was her mother's motto.

Tired of suppressing guilt, anger and heartache, she gave full rein to her emotions. She'd show her mother how to get the damn job done in a hurry! She gouged her sleepy horse, furiously swinging her rope. The startled horse began to buck, and Virginia felt a wave of sudden heat as the horse let out a squeal. She was trying to pull the horse's head up when she realized they had landed in the branding fire. The horse squealed again, more from fright than pain, and ran wildly. Virginia barely had time to shut her eyes as the horse hit the strands of wire full force.

She woke up a few minutes later on the ground. Great waves of nausea and remorse rolled through her. There was no excuse for her treatment of the horse. The thought that the horse might be injured sickened her.

"Do not move," was the heavily accented command she heard as she tried to turn her head toward Juan's voice. Juan had removed his shirt and was carefully placing it over her. She managed to see what was left of her shirt, tattered ribbons soaked in blood.

"The horse?" she managed to croak out.

"Señora has him. You lay still," was the terse reply.

Virginia struggled to sit up and clear her head, regardless of Juan's disapproval. She heard her mother's voice telling someone to take the horse to the barn, then passed out again.

Juan carefully lifted Virginia into the seat of a pickup as she regained her senses. She looked down and saw what little was left of her jeans as well. Juan grinned and shook his graying head. "I give you the shirt off my back," he said, "and now you want my pants, too, little one?"

Virginia tried to give Juan a smile in return, but only managed a sad replica. Blood was oozing and sticking the tattered clothing to her body. Another wave of nausea crashed over her.

Dolly finally appeared, sighing as she got into the truck and giving Juan strict orders about the injured horse and the still-waiting cattle. Virginia wanted to tell her she'd drive herself to the hospital if Dolly were too damn busy. Instead, she closed her eyes and felt the burning sting as tears rolled down her cheeks into the deep cuts of her neck. Dolly sped the truck up the embankment to the road, bouncing Virginia mercilessly.

"Does it hurt that bad?" she inquired. "You know you brought it on yourself. You should be feeling for that horse. His chest is ripped open, and there may be damage to the tendons in his legs."

Feeling too ill to reply, Virginia only nodded. Of course, she hated what she had done. And hated her weakness to stand up to her mother. The weakness that allowed her to lose control.

At the hospital, an elderly doctor told her she was "a lucky young lady," nearly severing some arteries. Through the welcome haze of painkillers, she wondered idly why hurt people were always "lucky." The doctor droned on about several days of bed rest, keeping the wounds and stitches clean and dry, and other instructions she mostly ignored.

On the way back to the ranch, Dolly began with, "I'm sure you'll be able to ride tomorrow. I've never let anything get in the way of work. That's what those pain pills are for. I just can't believe you pulled this when I need you the most."

Virginia tried to sound calm as she slowly formed the words in her mind and then lost them in the haze. She found them again as they slowly rose.

"I will be leaving tomorrow if I can sit up and drive," she said. "You have more than adequate help and you know it. I just can't be here anymore. It's time I got out on my own. Nothing I ever do is good enough, and I have discovered I don't like the person I become when I am around you."

"Oh, I see. You are trying to blame me for this wreck. That is just like you not to take responsibility for your own actions. After all I've done for you, this is my thanks?" shrieked Dolly.

"No, Mom. It's more like you to blame someone else. I can't change you, but I can change myself before I become another you. Someday, maybe, I will be good enough to meet your standards, but right now I'm not meeting my own. As you have so often pointed out, I will have big boots to fill some day. I just hope to God I can do it without hurting the people I love. Nothing, not this ranch, or everything that goes with it, is worth that."

Dolly stared silently ahead at the highway. She saw the tears streaming down her exhausted daughter's face out of the corner of her eye. She had never meant to hurt her daughter, or for the accident to happen, of course. She just had so much on her shoulders, too much to do. She was trying to prepare Virginia for the heavy responsibilities she'd inherit.

"I am sorry if you view me as a tyrant," Dolly said. "I love you, and have never intended to hurt you. I want you to realize that everything continues while you are away at school. The ranch is a huge enterprise, and I want you to be involved all you can. I think we are both too tired and drained to think. I just wanted you to be able to see what is going on, and be a part of it. Life isn't all college days, and maybe I am a little hard. But, I have to be to hold this place together.

Please don't leave. Let's talk this over in the morning."

Virginia couldn't remember her mother ever saying "please." She opened her eyes slightly. "The way I feel, I won't be going anywhere tomorrow," she said. "I just want to go to bed and try to rest, after I check on the horse. I sure hope the horse is going to be all right. They better have gotten those stockers done. We'd better check on that, too."

Dolly couldn't help but grin. "I'll go check on the horse and the cattle," she said. "You are going to go to bed, after a bowl of soup and a couple of pills."

Virginia had no idea she sounded just like her mother.

AMERICAN STOCKMAN

Stockman is an old term, one my Dad and Granddad used in place of rancher. I used it to define the difference created by ranchettes and 40-acre ranchers. This depicts the struggles we face.

I have fought many a battle
Skirmished over water and feed.
Scarred and wounded I start to bleed
For my heart is this war's chattel.

I have survived flood and drought
Watched helplessly as prices fell
Fought and gambled to no avail
Contending the voices of doubt.

I begin my day with the sun.
My body aches from abuses.
I see what labor produces.
I am in this for the long run.

I have ridden colts and old horses.
Miles and miles I have ridden
Across lands remote and forbidden
Yet bountiful in its resources.

I have witnessed death and birth
And given aid in both.
For this I live an oath
To respect life and Earth.

I struggle and still survive
Giving 'til I have no more
But, deep inside is the core
Of ancestors who thrive.

I cannot stop what has begun
For people want where I range
Believe that lives can be exchanged.
I am the American Stockman.

THE WRECK

The smell of fear, my stale sweat, horse sweat and cow manure clung to me. I glanced down at my wrinkled, stained clothes, clothes I had worn the day before, riding for miles through the dusty high desert, pushing cows, then working the cows in the corral, feeding hay, changing irrigation water and doing all the ranch chores I usually did. I had grabbed the clothes and boots off the floor last night when my teenaged daughters showed up injured from a car wreck. I was now in Salt Lake City, in the ICU, alone and frightened and far beyond the element I considered comfortable.

I had taken my first jet airplane ride, holding my semi-conscious daughter's hand while she lay on a stretcher, and was now surrounded by frantic activity, trying to squeeze against a wall, and in total disbelief any of this was real. I wanted to wake up and find myself back at the remote ranch, where our technology had not even met power poles.

My husband was on his way, setting things up at the ranch and taking my other daughter and son to their grandparents. It was now approaching noon, and I wondered why the four-hour trip was taking Doug so long.

A man in white stopped and stared, asking if I was all right — did I feel faint — while grabbing a chair for me. I explained with a dry, croaking voice I was waiting for news on my daughter, that Kelly had been whisked away behind the huge steel doors. He said he'd find out what was happening and handed me a cup of chlorinated city water I couldn't swallow. I closed my eyes and made promises to God I knew I couldn't keep.

The night flashed before me, scenes I didn't want to relive, didn't want to hear or remember. Waiting up for my twin seventeen-year-old daughters, showered, ready for bed and with a feeling of dread lying in the bottom of my stomach. Finally hearing the thumping and horn honking long before a single bobbing light came into view, drawing Doug and I out into the yard and road.

"They've gotten drunk and wrecked the damn car!" he swore. The car had been their Christmas gift, with the admonishing tag of, "Don't make us regret this!"

The car came limping up, still honking and almost beyond recognition. Teresa's long body climbed out from behind the wheel and came running, her face bloodied and eyes wild. "Don't kill us! Kelly is hurt!"

We ran to what was left of the passenger side, seeing Kelly's shoulder gashed in bloody stripes and her bobbing head as she tried to focus. The dented door couldn't be opened. We finally slid her out the back window, first knocking free the remaining shards of glass.

She was able to stand and we all made our way into the house. Kelly began to complain of her collarbone hurting, and Teresa's earlobe needed stitches. Seeing signs of shock, I used the cell phone we had gotten ten days earlier to call 911. I now remembered thanking God for finally having cell service, eliminating the twenty-five-mile trip to a phone. After arranging to meet the ambulance out on the highway, Dave ran out to unhook the stock trailer from the truck, as we had only one town-worthy vehicle.

I remembered the faces of the ambulance people, folks I knew and who had stayed at the local hospital with us for moral support. My twin girls hollering for them not to cut their new clothes and boots. Kelly yelling behind the white curtain in the ER, telling a doctor who inserted a catheter she "hated his gizzard" before quietly sobbing. I remembered going out, sitting on the curb, thinking I was going to throw up after I heard Kelly's neck was broken and she needed to be airlifted to Salt Lake City. That only one of us could go with her and Doug saying for me to go, that he'd get the other kids to my folks, and set up things at the ranch, then head for Salt Lake.

The man in white came back with a nurse following him. They'd taken Kelly for an MRI and the machine had broken down. She'd be out in a while. I nodded that I understood and closed my eyes again.

More scenes came back, Teresa recounting the story of losing control on the seven-mile dirt road to the ranch, not sure of how many times the car rolled after shooting off the road. How when it finally came to rest, Kelly wouldn't wake up and Teresa began running back to the highway a few miles away for help for her twin sister until a voice spoke to her, a voice telling her to turn around and go back, to start the car she didn't believe was drivable. Teresa obeyed the voice, turned around and ran back toward the car to find Kelly out of her head, stumbling in the sage. She got her twin sister back into the car by having her climb in the back, through the open window. Teresa found the keys still in the ignition, prayed a silent prayer and turned the key. The little broken car rumbled to life. Teresa grabbed the wheel and began to drive, intent on getting her sister to the ranch and to help.

The nurse reappeared with some men, all wearing physicians' uniforms with accompanying badges bearing various names before the MD letters, telling me my daughter was being placed in a room and I'd be able to see her soon. They then gravely explained she'd had a terrific blow to the head. There was brain swelling, so the MRI view was limited, and they couldn't see clearly if there was substantial damage. There were broken vertebrae in her neck, and she'd suffered some paralysis since arriving. We'd need to discuss what was to be done.

I explained my husband was on his way. Couldn't any decisions wait a short while for his arrival? They agreed to wait and then led me to a room where machines surrounded my daughter, with lines leading to her. They tried to prepare me for the sight of her face and head, grossly swollen and bruised almost beyond recognition. Steroids were being administered to help reduce the swelling.

I was asked to step out and found my place against the wall, where I once again prayed that wall would open up and magically transport Kelly and me back to the ranch, where we could act as if this was all just a bad dream. A woman approached me, asking if I had gotten a room or had somewhere to stay, since I was not allowed to stay overnight at the hospital. She studied my face and asked when I'd eaten last. I glanced out a window and was shocked to see dusk falling. As I glanced back to the woman, I saw Doug hurrying toward me. As he reached my side, the team of doctors came out of Kelly's room and asked us to follow them so we could talk. Poor Doug learned the full extent of our daughter's injuries the hardest way possible.

One of our options for the broken neck was a halo, a device to keep Kelly's head and neck immobile for a few months. The halo encircled her head and was secured by drilling bolts into our daughter's skull with braces attached to a hard plastic, lamb-fleeced vest. The second option was an operation, using bone from her body or a donor's to replace the crushed vertebrae. Both carried their respective risks. We voted for the halo, hoping to avoid problems for Kelly later in life. The paralysis was temporary, they believed. They would run more scans when the swelling in her brain went down. She was heavily sedated and would remain so until the morning. We were to get some rest after checking on her.

Doug and I found a room near the hospital. He went out to find some food. It had been more than twenty-four hours since I had eaten and he hadn't exactly been filling up at the all-you-can-eat buffet. I had managed to hold it all together, barely. I steeled myself for the call I needed to make to my folks. I'd lost an older sister to a car wreck when she was in high school. I knew they were worried sick, and I'd have to reassure them. Doug could call his family when he returned. He had grabbed clothes at the ranch for us both, and I stepped into the shower, numb to the water temperature and the silent tears that fell.

Early the next morning, we hurried to our daughter's room. She saw us, called "Mom!' and begin sobbing. It broke our hearts, but we calmed her, keeping our emotions under control. We explained about the injuries and what we believed to be the best option. While her activities, like riding and school, would be curtailed for a few months, she could eventually return to them.

A new doctor appeared, and said they were ready to place the halo. We could follow them to the room where the procedure would take place, he said, but would probably prefer to wait outside while the holes were drilled through Kelly's skull. The sooner her neck was stabilized, the less chance for paralysis. We waited outside the room, willing our senses to stop hearing the whir, to ignore the smell of the drill going through her skull. I had been instructed in keeping the drilled holes clean and understood its importance. I was trying hard to convince myself I could get us through all this.

Back in Kelly's cubby of the ICU, a vibrant, red-haired teenager appeared and introduced herself as Robin, a friend of the girls we hadn't met. We knew her cousins, aunts and uncles. She lived in the area and her parents offered their home to us.

The cell phone began to ring and neighbors who lived at least thirty miles away from our ranch began to call. They wanted to haul the cattle they'd heard we had corralled to the sale for us. They'd lined up people and equipment to begin cutting our wild hay. Someone else offered to keep the wells on the range going. What else could they do besides pray? Where were the other kids, and could they keep them for us? Our already ravaged emotions were barely contained at their generous offers as we gratefully assured them we'd be home in a few days, that Doug had turned the cattle out, and that the meadows needed to dry some. We knew they would put our work before their own.

A therapist came in, explaining that Kelly would need to start walking that afternoon and that she would show us how to help her and how to adjust to life for the next few months. It was imperative Kelly not fall; it could cause paralysis or even death. I would be responsible for helping her use the restroom, bathe, and even eat. The vest could never be wet. Kelly could be sponge-bathed only above the waist.

I eyed Kelly's heavy, waist-length hair and wondered how I'd keep her pride and joy clean. The weight of the halo threw her balance out of kilter and she didn't have the luxury of moving her head even a fraction of an inch. I would feed her since her plate would not be visible to her unless lifted to eye level.

The vest could not be moved or removed; adjustments would be performed only at the hospital. The vest, resembling something a female superhero would wear, would become uncomfortable, but there could be no scratching, as any cut would quickly become infected and remain undetected until the vest's removal months from now. I could thread an alcohol-soaked towel thru the openings for relief and cleanliness. We would need to buy extra-large, button-up shirts to accommodate the vest and halo.

Kelly was wheeled back in, sobbing quietly. This kid who never cried had shed more tears in the last twenty-four hours than she had in her entire lifetime. I tried to find a way to put my arms around her, but was afraid of jarring the bars that ran from her chest to her skull. I simply slid my head between the bars and laid my head on her now rock-hard chest, squeezing her hand. We encouraged her to rest, assuring her we'd be there. Her greatest fear was typical of a ranch-raised kid: she didn't want to be alone in such a strange place. She fell asleep gripping my hand.

We learned how to do everyday tasks, accommodating for the halo, over the next few days. Robin came faithfully every day, bringing small gifts, and encouraging us to leave Kelly's bedside for a few minutes while Kelly slept. Robin would be right there if she woke. Robin's parents kept the offer of their home open to us. We finally slipped out one day to walk around the hospital and feel the sun. Bouquet after bouquet of flowers began to fill the room, until we were asked to remove some.

We bought pillows to surround Kelly for the long ride home. Any jarring caused her excruciating pain. Simply getting her in and out of a vehicle proved to be a major undertaking. Months later, I would get her into an old ranch truck and be unable to get her out without Doug's help.

Buster, our seven-year-old son, and Teresa came running when we pulled into the yard. I had cautioned both not to stare, and said she'd need all of us for support. They hung back, Teresa finally coming and holding her twin in her arms as they both sobbed. Buster watched carefully, then came running, wrapping his little arms around his big sister's legs. Doug and I felt tears of love welling up as we looked at each other.

Kelly insisted on seeing her horse before going in the house. I showed Teresa how to help her sister walk as we made our way to the pasture. Kelly's horse came up, bringing his head over the fence. He stared at her and widened his nostrils, and evidently didn't like any of it. He reached over, grabbed one of the halo bars in his teeth, and began to shake it, pulling Kelly almost off her feet. Doug reached up and slugged him squarely in the face. I went weak in the knees, felt sick at my stomach as I tried to support Kelly, and was grateful steady-minded Teresa was supporting Kelly on the other side. The doctors would have probably fainted on the spot. I quickly checked Kelly out while the horse stared at us. There appeared to be no damage.

That evening, after I had settled everyone into their beds, I reflected on the last few days. We would face many tears and trials over the next few months, but were blessed to have our daughter not permanently disabled, our family and our lifestyle — a lifestyle that means loving your neighbor like yourself, no matter the distance.

SACRAMENTO MOUNTAIN SPIRITS

When I ride in these mountains, it seems I can feel the spirits of the past around me. I think whatever horse I'm riding feels them, as well. I always cherish the bit of pottery, the arrowhead, the purple glass or concho I may find.

I roam these mountains searching for sign
Hoping to find favor from the divine.
We paint our pots black and white
Grow our maize and crops in sight
Of our villages along the waterway
That diminishes even while we pray.

I roam these mountains in heavy armor
Proudly on horses, not a peon farmer.
We ride to conquer and bring God's word
To find riches and a trail for the herds
Destined for the Church at Santa Fe
Following the Sacramento on my way.

I roam these mountains on deerskin-clad feet
Riding and looting, hunting for meat
Leading men dressed in blue places
Where cliffs end in towering spaces
With no fuel to burn, no water to drink
Where they will die, left to rot and stink.

I roam these mountains riding in deep shade
Following faint trails game have made
Making caches of cinch rings and stolen goods
In hidden camps deep in these woods
Always watching, wary of anyone I see.
I am a wanted man and will never be free.

I roam these mountains tending cattle
Acknowledging they are not my chattel
Feeling the spirits of the tinctured past
Drifting by in roles eternally cast
Grateful for time allotted in this land
Rising above the glistening White Sand.

63

SNOWY RIDE

I am cold, colder than a man should be and still be alive. I felt my body begin to draw up into itself hours ago, leaving a physical space between the first of many layers I wear and my tightened skin. It no longer hurts to breathe the frozen air and my legs and arms don't ache any longer. They are now like wooden stumps that slowly, mechanically, respond to my wishes. I am tired, beyond tired, but must continue lifting my heavy head to make sure the horse under me is still going the right direction. I trust him, but only somewhat. He became a little confused earlier.

But, let me start my story from the beginning. It has snowed relentlessly for days, with temperatures hovering around zero, give or take ten degrees. Our fuel tanks are near empty, and our haystacks are shrinking too rapidly because of this massive storm that continues to swirl above us. The fuel must come first; we need it to get feed to the cattle. The additional hay must also come, but can wait a little while.

The ranch is isolated, with no electricity, fifteen miles from the nearest phone, and ten miles from the nearest neighbor or paved road, which is a U.S. highway. It is to this neighbor I am riding, hoping to get a ride, a ride in a vehicle, to the phone at the roadside store five miles further. We keep a freezer there and my wife has asked me to fill my saddlebags with meat since we ran out several days ago. While the ranch sits nestled on a county road, we're the last on a long list to get plowed. It will be weeks before we hear the sound of a county plow. "County-maintained" means grading once a year and snow removal once or twice a year, after all the other roads are in good shape.

I left my worried wife and children to feed the cattle and horses when we decided this ride must be made and that I must ride back in the same day. My wife was empathic about the timing of the return ride, because no one except she and the kids knew I was going, and no one would know if I didn't make it. She has a vivid imagination and I knew she had mental images of me lying frozen on the snow, dead eyes iced over. If I haven't returned by an hour after dark, my wife will saddle up and begin searching for me, leaving our teenager in charge of her younger brother. No one could survive a night in this high desert country during this cold storm. This winter has broken the grip of the devastating drought, but is a nightmare for ranchers tending stock already weakened from short, sparse grass.

I rode out the ranch gate this morning and up the slight rise to the small flat that gradually ascends into the foothills before the pass. The snow lay in drifts like sugared mounds, ranging from three to six feet with ground swept bare in places by the eternal wind. The howling wind filled the air around me and I pulled my scarf up to cover my face. As I neared the pass and the protection of the trees, the snow lay deeper with less rise in the drifts. At times, Yellar used his big chest to break a trail through the deepening snow.

Suddenly my horse fell directly out from under me. I managed to stay over him, a couple feet above the saddle. He shook his big head and wallered out of the gully that the snow had filled and hidden. I loosened my big snow pacs from the stirrups, knowing I'd never get them out if he fell. Cold sweat broke on my body, trapped in the layers padding me. Grimly, I gathered my reins in my bulky mittens and rode on.

After several more startling, heart-racing drops into hidden gullies, we topped the pass into the next valley. I should have been able to spot the distant neighbor's ranch and the highway, but ground blizzards swirled below me like an evil magician's trick. Yellar began sliding. I tried to help by leaning back to get my weight off his front end, and turned toward the direction of the ranch. The horse was now soaked with salty sweat, his head bent down in fatigue. I reached to rub his neck with a stiff arm, transmitting my thanks and encouragement. A big, startlingly fast horse, he was bought for the kids to rope off and barrel race in high school rodeos, but he had shown various signs of possessing low intelligence. I was grateful for the heart he'd shown today.

Suddenly, Yellar threw his head up and neighed, staring straight ahead. I peered through the swirling snow and could see nothing. A few moments later, I saw the outline of the large trees at the neighbor's ranch. Feeling a surge of energy, I straightened in the saddle and began working my toes and fingers to try and regain some feeling. Yellar gathered himself up under me and picked up his pace, throwing snow out from under us like a machine.

We crossed what we knew had to be the highway, yet it was so covered by snow, only the occasional snow marker standing above a drift made it recognizable. The fence bordering it was nowhere to be seen, completely buried in the snow. We rode up the lane to the ranch yard, Yellar neighing at a place he'd never been or seen before. Wood smoke drifted on the air, making me shiver as I thought of the warmth of a fire. I stiffly dismounted, stomping feeling back into my legs as I put the horse in the barn, giving him hay and grain and a chance to rest.

No one had appeared, so I walked to the neighbor's pickup and felt the hood, which was still warm. All four wheels were chained up. My neighbor must be out feeding with his team of horses, I reasoned. The keys were in the truck and I drove out, headed for the highway and the store five miles down the road. The heater felt like heaven and I delighted in its warmth. The highway was a mess of drifts, with only my neighbor's tracks sliced through. I was beginning to wonder if I was in a nightmare and if we were part of a handful of people still alive in a world gone white and frozen.

I made it to the store, where another neighbor and the store owners were gathered around the stove, excited to see me. No one was venturing out in this weather, none of the usual tourists clad in shorts wanting to know why the desert was this cold and why it was snowing. My neighbors had been making plans to reach us. I drank hot coffee shoved into my hands, the steam melting my frozen mustache, while assuring them the family was all right, although we were out of fuel.

I called my worried father-in-law, who had already hired a bulldozer to make a trail into the ranch and check on our well-being. I arranged for him to coordinate the dozer and fuel truck. I grabbed candy bars and jerky to eat on the way, explaining I couldn't accept the worried offers of dinner and a bed, but had to hurry to begin the ride home. I filled my saddlebags with Polish sausages, remembering my family's plea for meat and thinking my wife would stretch them into various meals.

I returned to the neighbor's ranch, parking his truck as I found it, scrawling a note of thanks to place on the seat. Yellar had eaten his meal, and nickered at me. I resaddled him and led him out of the protection of the barn. We both heaved a big sigh as we looked at the vast area we had to recross.

The temperature was beginning to fall in anticipation of the coming night. Dark came early in January and the clouds now sat on the ground, adding to the density of the blowing snow. I had hoped the wind would begin to die, but it appeared to be gaining force.

As we crossed the highway and began the gradual climb back up the pass, I prayed Yellar didn't sink through the snow to become tangled in the buried fence. Our tracks I had planned to follow were gone, drifted over. I was trying to remember where a particularly deep gully was when we fell straight down several feet, causing me to do the splits above the saddle before landing hard back in it. My groin muscles screamed in protest and the horse stood dazed for a moment before he shook his big head and began trying to climb out.

I kicked my feet free of the stirrups and leaned forward to help him. The walls were too close to allow me to get off and I feared he might pin me while struggling out. He plowed ahead, once again using his wide chest to break a trail. We continued on, Yellar with his head now close to the ground, sniffing. Maybe he wasn't as dumb as we all thought. Like a bloodhound, the old buggar was trying to sniff our earlier path.

I knew we were going to be in trouble. The sun was lowering behind the heavy veil of gray and I wasn't cold any longer, just tired, and kept nodding off to be rudely jolted awake when we fell through a drift. I tried to focus on my wife and kids' faces.

I am past the point where I began this story. I am vaguely worried that my wife is preparing to ride out to find me, and afraid she won't make it far before becoming lost or falling into a gully. Darkness is slowly surrounding us, comforting somehow, and adding to my exhausted state. I am fighting all my senses to stay awake, to stay alert as the big horse plods on and on, first traveling evenly, then jarring me to my teeth as we fall through drift after drift. The ride and the night are eternal.

Suddenly Yellar stops abruptly, almost knocking me from the saddle, throws his head high, and takes huge, deep sniffs of air. He begins whinnying and becomes excited, lifting his huge, snow-caked feet high to strike out quickly at a much faster pace. It has shaken me awake, and I become aware of a slight smell on the now still air. Is it piñon smoke?

I am almost afraid to think of it, afraid I might be dreaming, and try to push away thoughts of my warm home and my family. But the horse lifts those feet up and slams them down, breaking half-round balls of ice free from his feet. He wants to travel faster, but is afraid of falling or slipping. Then I hear it, the answer to Yellar's whinny. Then the howling, barking chorus of our dogs. I close my eyes as tears form, silently thanking God we have made it. We are almost home! My next thought is that darkness has fallen. Has my wife ridden out and missed us, or is the answering whinny I thought I heard coming from her horse?

I have reached the rise above the house and see the weak yellow glow of kerosene in our windows. A flashlight appears by the corrals and barn, and we half slip, half slide on the lane down to the light. My daughter is standing by my wife, holding in her hands a halter. She throws it to the ground as she grabs my horse's bridle.

My wife quickly moves to stand beside me, telling me to get down, that our daughter will take care of the horse. I brace against her shoulder as I try to get my right foot to move, to kick free of the stirrup. She moves to that side to break away the ice, then slowly forces my boot out of the stirrup. She repeats the same on the left side, then says quietly to try to get off. She is deadly calm, a warning sign to me. I know I must be bad and she reaches up to place her arms around me and begins to gently pull me toward her while my daughter holds the horse's head, staring at her parents with eyes like my grandmother's blue china saucers.

I don't remember losing the reins, but my daughter has them, I discover. My wife silently shakes her head at me, and resumes gradually pulling me down to her. Yellar is tall and she stretches upward, trying to slowly take my weight against her strong shoulders. I half fall against her, feel her brace herself and take the jolt as I try to stand. She wraps her arms more securely around me and tells me to be still, to let the blood circulate for a moment.

I am home and I am safe. The road will be opened tomorrow, and the cattle will get feed. My daughter has found the sausages and shows them to her mother. I couldn't know that the road would blow closed again the next night, and that it would take a few years before any of us could even look at a Polish sausage, but that's another story.

COW COUNTRY CODE

There's always been a code of honor among cow people, helping
neighbors, doing the right thing, even if it's done begrudgingly.

> I listened carefully, listened to directions
> All based on recollections
> Of cattle last seen, water and grass green.
>
> His face was lined, lined from a lifetime
> Of counting every nickel and dime.
> Worries and cares, hopes and prayers.
>
> He'd outlived his child, outlived his wife
> Seemed to have tired of life.
> After the stroke, spirit and body broke.
>
> Drought had fallen, fallen heavy on the land
> Grass replaced by piles of sand.
> Tanks lay long dry, under a blazing sky.
>
> We prowled around, prowled for his cows
> Swore to ourselves renewed vows
> Of helping neighbors, and our free labor.
>
> But, we faced mortality, faced our own years
> And sought to appease our fears
> Of growing old, and outfits sold.

Cattle were gathered, gathered and sorted
Numbers tallied and reported.
We figured the amount, he was given the count.

It would be enough, would buy a place in town
To watch the sun go down
On a quiet street, with memories bittersweet.

His old hand shook, shook as the paper curled
That gave a dollar amount to his world.
He took our word, couldn't really see the herd.

That tally he held, held with quiet pride
Was one time we all lied.
We'd padded the count, added to the amount.

His cattle were thin, were rough and open
Hadn't calved like we were hopin'.
We added a few, ours, and he never knew.

It was our raising, raised to do right
In the old days of black and white
No question of gray, only one right way.

We rode hard, hard and long all day
For something more valued than pay
A time honored code, for this we rode.

SPIRIT OF GIVING

Snow lay in heavy drifts, cedar and juniper trees frosted with thick icing, while icicles hung nearly to the ground from the ranch house roof. It was a silent, isolated world, one we had grown accustomed to. But our old house, snuggled in its setting of giant, ancient elms where the broad valley and foothills of the towering mountains met, was cozy on this Christmas Eve, fragrant from the piñon tree decorated with homemade ornaments and the smell of cinnamon and other spices from holiday baking.

The wood stove crackled and popped, radiating warmth against the subzero temperatures. The soft, yellowed glow of propane and kerosene lights fell on the pigtailed twin girls bent over a board game on the table. I wished they'd hurry up and finish the game so I could put the finishing touches on the little dolls I had bought, dolls for which I was making fancy dresses.

It would be a sparse Christmas. We'd had a rough year on the ranch and most of the girls' gifts were handmade by their father and me. The money we did get came the same day the snow started, and we didn't even try to travel the ninety miles to town. Cattle had to be pulled off the range and brought home abruptly. According to our radio, most roads were closed.

I was about to tell the girls to start putting things away and get ready for bed when Dave and I heard the deep silence of the cold night broken as the dogs began barking and the sound of a vehicle growled in the distance. We exchanged worried looks, wondering why someone was so desperate to get to us, to break through fifteen miles of bumper-deep drifts on a dirt road on Christmas Eve.

We had no phone or electric lines. News came from neighbors, who relayed messages from the only phone, thirty miles away. Dave pulled on his winter boots, wound his scarf round his neck and shrugged into his heavy coat while the girls tried to scrape ice off the windows to see who was arriving. We feared what news our desperate visitor might bring.

Dave stepped out on the porch as the truck came to rest in front of the house, saying over his shoulder, "It's Kitt! What on earth?"

Kitt was our nearest neighbor, an old bachelor whose kids had grown and left home. In the back of his snow-covered truck was a piñon tree, and he carried a large box as he made his way to the house through the deep snow.

"Didn't know if I was gonna make it!" he exclaimed, stomping snow and ice off his boots. "I had to get a tree since my youngest came home, and needed to spread some Christmas cheer to my neighbors," he explained as he set the box on the table.

Kitt knew it was a rough year for everyone and wasn't about to let our little girls not have a good Christmas, no matter what it took. He gave the girls bright packages, directing them to open them, if they wished. He handed us a huge box of chocolates, and brought out a bottle of "something to knock the chill off, if we had some glasses." We toasted the holiday and the spirit of giving as the girls unwrapped bright silk scarves, warm mittens and sweet treats.

My daughters will always remember the kind neighbor who broke a trail to the ranch so they could have a better Christmas, and we will never forget Kitt's spirit of giving when none of us had much to give besides the greatest gift, love for our neighbors.

PRAYERS

While we were ranching in Butte Valley, Nevada, our valley caught fire. At one point, three sides of the valley were on fire, the Medicines, the Cherries and the Delker mountain ranges all blazing. It was another year of severe drought. We didn't lose any cattle, but our neighbor did. This is another case of being careful of what you pray for.

We prayed for rain, prayed for snow.
The prayers were but an empty echo
Returning to taunt again and again
As springs dried and cattle grew thin.

Searching for cattle, searching for feed
On horses weary and weak-kneed
We became gritty, dry as the land
Cracked and parched as the blowing sand.

We watched clouds gather, and gather more
Shadows darkening the valley floor
Followed by silence so profound
Shattered by a drop striking ground.

We shouted for joy, shouted in fear
As sounds of thunder drew near.
Lightning came in its wake
Unfurling like a blacksnake.

We saw it strike, and strike again
Smelled the smoke on the wind
Heard the wind lift and rise
To help her ally from the skies.

Deanna Dickinson McCall

The grass burned hot, and hotter still
A red swath cutting down the hill
Consuming all in its path
Exploding trees in its wrath.

We spurred our mounts, and spurred again
Driving cattle before the wind
Blindly whirling in the smoke
Every breath a ragged choke.

The heavens opened, and opened wider
Drenching every cow and rider.
Dry earth became a quagmire
As death was dealt to the fire.

We climbed the ridge, and climbed some more
Turned to look through the downpour.
As the fire gave a final roar,
Lay smoldering on the valley floor.

Cattle were counted, and recounted
While the knots in our bellies mounted.
We were short, out a few
But had done what we could do.

We pushed the cattle, and pushed them more
Their sorry hides scorched and sore
On horses cloaked in suds and sweat
Knowing God's wrath we had met.

We watched the skies clear, and clear again
And hung our heads with the sin
Of our answered prayer that day
And watched our storm drift away.

ELENA'S ANGELS

The roan horse nickered softly in recognition as the petite, dark-haired girl approached. It was late afternoon, and the horse had been waiting for the daily ritual.

Like the girl, the horse was fine-boned, almost fragile-looking, both showing Spanish ancestry in their features. Slipping a pole down, the girl entered the crude corral made by her and her father. Speaking quietly in the horse's ear, she vaulted smoothly onto his back. Using her knees, she guided him toward the opening where she had lowered the pole. In one fluid movement, the horse, and the girl who seemed to become part of the horse, leapt over the remaining poles.

"Are you going to saddle him, Elena?" asked her father as he came limping out of the old trailer house they called home. Manuel looked at his daughter with pride. Manuel had felt proud lately. Hadn't he been able to buy this land, and put a home on it? Soon he would have the money to pay for a well, and then they would even have running water.

"Yes, Papa. Then I will set the poles up and the barrels." She pointed with her delicate chin toward the flat area she used for an arena. Father and daughter had cleared the area of brush using mattocks and shovels, making an area clear of obstacles for Elena to practice her rodeo events. The ground resembled cement more than a real arena, but at least it was level.

Pushing a bleating nanny goat out of the way, the girl went to the old horse trailer her father had traded for fence work and began to pull out her tack. While she saddled her horse, Manuel led the heavy-bagged nanny to the ramp and stanchion, and brought a foal out of a wire pen to nurse the goat. The foal's mother had died. Manuel took in other people's orphaned foals to raise. The small amount he charged helped to keep beans on the table when his disability check wasn't enough.

Manuel worried about his daughter. She wanted to go into town and enter the junior rodeo. He knew school wasn't easy for her. He had heard the kids on the bus making fun of their place, calling it "Fort Apache." He knew his proud daughter would never let him know when things were hard, but he had heard her cry at night, her attempts to muffle the sound not effective through the paper thin walls of the old trailer. He had come here to start a new life for them, but it seemed no matter how far north they went the prejudice was always there. He was tired of "wetback" jokes, and so tired of swallowing his pride it rose like bile at times, threatening to gag him. He was born in this country, loved it enough to have left part of his leg in a Viet Nam jungle.

Elena was lining up her horse to make a barrel run. Both horse and rider needed to have their undivided attention focused on the first barrel. A race left no room for errors. Manuel pulled out his pocket-watch to time her. A stopwatch would be nice, but out of their budget. Powdery white dust rose at the gate, and a pickup pulled in as Manuel watched Elena finish her run.

"Que paso, Manuel?" asked the neighbor as he climbed out of his truck. "Is Elena going to the rodeo in town?" The tall, lanky rancher shook Manuel's work-worn hand.

"Yes, Mr. Brown. She wanted to enter the queen contest as well, but that would be a waste of time. Her mother could have sewn her fancy clothes for it. But me, I am no sewer. And we cannot afford such things."

"I see the dust raisin' every evening and knew something was going on. Elena is a good hand with a horse. She can get more out of one than most folks." He didn't add his thought of how little she had to work with.

"I just came by to see how the foal is doing and will get out of your way. I may have some work for you next week, if you are interested. I have some more fence needin' fixin'."

"I will come by, Mr. Brown. As you can see, the foal is doing well. Nothing like a goat's milk to raise a foal."

"Adios, Manuel. And tell Elena good luck."

Mr. Brown pulled his hat down to block the afternoon sun as he drove past the girl and the little horse. They made a pretty picture, but he couldn't imagine Elena and her mustang-type, grass-fed horse would have a chance against those expensive Quarter Horses, professionally trained and kept on careful diets. He had watched Elena when she worked for him, helping on the roundups, and at brandings. She had a way with horses. Probably goes back to the old Spanish blood, he mused.

The next day, Manuel picked Elena up from school as he had to be in town to pay for the rodeo entries. Manuel had a hard time refusing his daughter anything, and she had won the argument about the rodeo. They stopped at the truck stop to fill up the old truck and Elena ran in to pay for the gas. The nice lady was there again, the plump redhead whose name was Carol. She asked Elena about her horse and if she was still riding for the ranchers in the valley. Elena told her about how well her horse was doing, and that she was going to pay her entries as soon as they were done there. She added proudly she was not only entering the girls' events, she was going to try for the queen contest.

Carol took the money Elena carefully counted out. The girl's eyes shone as she spoke of the rodeo. Carol knew things were tough for the girl and her father. She wished there was something she could do to help them. Carol told her she would come watch her if she got the day off. As she watched Elena walk out to the old pickup, the other cashier came in.

"How's it going, Carol?" the heavy brunette asked as she came behind the counter. She followed Carol's absentminded gaze out the window. "That the little girl you told me about?" she asked.

"Yea, that's her, Judy. I just feel so bad. She is wantin' to enter the queen contest in that darn rodeo, and you know how those kids will be. She and her poor ol' dad don't have money for fancy clothes. It will be bad enough with her just showing up on that little horse. It don't matter a bit she can outride any of them. Kids can be so cruel."

Judy watched Carol's blue eyes water at the thought of what the poor little girl would go through. She knew Carol had firsthand experience at being poor and growing up without a mother.

"Well, girl, instead of just standing there, let's do something. I'll talk to the manager and the other clerks. I bet we can at least get together enough money to get her a neat outfit, and maybe a matching saddle blanket."

Manuel had paid the witcher to come, even though the well driller didn't believe in witching. The shriveled old man was tapping the ground with his forked willow stick.

"Here. Here is where the water lays," the witcher said. "Lotsa water. Don't let that driller go anywhere else." He looked up with a nearly toothless grin. It was good to have someone respect his talent, even if it was a poor old Mexican, he thought. At least they knew the value of water.

"I want that big goat over there." He shook his divining rod at a large brown goat, his payment for finding water.

Manuel heard the sound of the school bus brakes as it pulled off the highway. He headed for the goat the old man had chosen.

Elena saw her father loading a goat into the old man's pickup, tying it to the side. She went into the trailer and sat down on the old couch. Dust rose and she sighed. It was hard to keep house when water was hauled in barrels. Hard enough to try and keep herself clean, she thought. She got up and stirred the chile her father had on the stove. The fragrance made her stomach rumble.

She would change from her school clothes and get ready to ride. She carefully folded her jeans and shirt. She could get another day out of them. She would wait a day or two and then wear them. She was always careful to keep her few good clothes unstained, and never wore them after school. She knew the reason her father didn't want her to be in the queen contest was because the other girls would have fancy new clothes. Even though most of the contest was supposed to be scored on horsemanship, the clothes counted for a lot. The judges always picked girls who wore expensive outfits. She would show them all she could ride, and next year she would save the money somehow to buy such clothes, she resolved. Right now she needed to get out and practice, she chided herself.

"Elena, are you coming out or not?" her father yelled. "I have the horse here for you."

Elena came out in her old work clothes, clothes that were hand-me-downs from a local ranchers' children.

"Who was that man, Papa?" she asked as she took the horse from her father.

"That was a well-witcher. He says we will have a good well, a very good well. Maybe even enough to irrigate with, Elena."

Elena watched her father's face light up with hope. She felt a bad feeling in the pit of her stomach. She had seen her father's hopes and dreams fail so often. He placed too much faith in the old ways. It was hard for her to watch these things, and a little of him, die each time things failed.

"Do you have the watch ready, Papa?" She changed the subject as she climbed on the horse to warm him up.

Elena rode the little horse around, walking, then trotting him, before going into a smooth lope that sent her hair flying to the sides like a raven's wings. She could feel everything about the little horse. Their rhythm was one. Her heart and his hard little hooves kept perfect time.

A car pulled into their road. Father and daughter watched as it neared.

"Who is it, Papa?"

Manuel squinted through the dust. He had no idea who would drive a car out to see them. Probably someone lost or having car trouble, he thought.

As the car pulled up Elena recognized the driver.

"It is the lady from the gas station, Papa."

"Why would she come out here, Elena? What can she want?" Manuel worried.

Carol got out of the car. She smiled at Elena, noting the ragged clothes the girl wore, though her natural beauty showed in the smile she returned to Carol. Manuel came limping up, and respectfully greeted the visitor.

"You must be getting excited about the rodeo, Elena. Only two more days! I see you are practicing." Carol stood leaning against the car while Manuel waited patiently to see what this visit was about.

"Oh, yes, ma'm. We will be ready."

"I have something for you, Elena. Maybe this will help with the rodeo," said Carol as she opened the back door to the car. She brought out a large box all tied in ribbons and bows.

Elena slid off the horse gracefully, barely touching the ground.

"For me?" she asked shyly.

"Yes, we just wanted to do something for you. You are a good girl, Elena. We all wish you lots of luck, too. Now open it!"

Elena looked at her father. He nodded. She carefully untied the bows and opened the box. A beautiful red blouse lay folded, all sequins and pearls with fringe. Underneath lay a pair of jeans, girl jeans, not the cheap boys' style she always wore. And in the bottom was a felt hat, black with a red edging around the brim. They were brand new, the tags still attached.

Elena felt her throat close as tears filled her eyes. Manuel smiled at his daughter.

"Aren't you going to thank her, Elena?" he gently chided. "She will think I raised you with no manners."

"Yes, Papa. I, I just don't know what to say," she stammered through her tears. Elena ran her rough yet delicate hands over the fabric of the blouse. She had never even dared to dream of such things.

"Thank you so much. But, why would you do this for me? I don't understand."

"Sometimes, Elena, people need a little help. The people who work at the store saw that. We all want the best for you, and we all will be there to watch you. Oops, I almost forgot!" Carol reached into the car again.

"Here is a pad to make your outfit complete," she said, handing the black and red saddle pad to Elena and hugging the sobbing girl all at the same time. Manuel saw tears in Carol's blue eyes as she held his daughter.

"I thank all of you," he said. "You have made a dream come true for my daughter."

The next day the driller came, having arrived at an agreement with Manuel. He would take the down payment Manuel had given him and pray that Manuel would continue to make the small payments they had agreed to. He knew he was a sucker, but he honestly wanted to help the crippled Mexican and his daughter. Living without running water could be miserable, especially when winter began.

Gene got out of his drilling rig and waited for Manuel to make his way through the goats, chickens and cats that blocked his path.

"Need some more critters, Manuel?" he asked with a grin.

Manuel shook his head. "They are a pain sometimes. But, almost all of them make good tamales!" he answered, laughing.

Then, soberly he said, "Gene, I want you to drill right over here. Where I have placed the stick." He pointed to a small mounded area.

"Right there, huh, Manuel?"

"Yes. I think we will find good, sweet water right there. And not so deep. Maybe so shallow I won't owe you any more money!" Manuel teased.

"It's your money. I will pull over there, Manuel."

Manuel prayed a fervent prayer while he watched Gene set up the rig. He limped over when Gene seemed in position.

Manuel watched the drilling begin, praying harder and harder. The old cable tool rig was loud, screeching and banging as the drill cut into the earth, searching for Manuel's dream. The rig was slow and outdated. The summer day wore on, until Gene hollered and waved at Manuel.

"Here we go, Manuel! Water!"

Manuel limped over, thanking God for answering his prayer as he neared the rig.

"We've got water, and not very deep," Gene said. "You won't have to have too big a pump, if this is what I hope it is. I just don't know if we are really in the table. Let me go down some more and see what happens." Gene looked a little confused. He had expected to go much deeper.

The rig began drilling again when suddenly a roar filled the air. Water shot far up into the air, soaking both men and the rig. The animals all ran, setting up a clamor that equaled the sound of the released water.

The men looked at each other dumbly, then grabbed each other, dancing in a circle of mud and water.

"Oh, my God! Oh, my God!" Gene yelled. "I just can't friggin' believe it!"

"'My God' is right. He is answering my prayers," Manuel said, suddenly solemn. He drew the sign of the cross across his chest and let his tears flow as unashamedly as the bountiful flow of new water.

Gene had never had the experience of hitting an artesian well and added his silent prayers to Manuel's. He hoped it would stay, that it wasn't a fluke. If anyone deserved a break, it was this man in front of him.

"Manuel, if this stays going 'til morning, it is for real," Gene said, eyeing the water now flowing up like a gentle fountain.

"It is real. It is the answer to my prayers. You do not question God's gifts," Manuel stated levelly.

The morning sun was just a suggestion of rose and yellow when Elena woke. She lay in her bed, thinking about the last few days. Good things were happening to her and her father. She arose and threw on the clothes she had worn the previous day after school. Washing and brushing her horse would be a cold, messy job. She eyed the new clothes she would wear before changing for the rodeo. She still couldn't believe it, that she owned such things.

Manuel watched his petite daughter empty the buckets of water she had hauled to her horse. She would come inside and clean up soon. She was toweling the horse dry when he called to her.

"Elena, you had better come in and get ready. Andale!" he called from the open door. Her breakfast of freshly gathered, then scrambled, eggs and homemade tortillas was waiting on the stove.

"Coming, Papa. I'm almost done," she called back.

Elena was not hungry, but also knew better than to waste food. She rolled her eggs into the tortilla and placed it in her coat pocket for later. Right now her stomach was far too nervous for food.

She had hauled water the night before from the new "fountain," as she called it, and had heated it to bathe. She and Manuel would find more work and save enough to buy pipe to run the water into their trailer, maybe before winter came, if their luck continued.

The flag rippled in the wind as Manuel stood with his hat over his heart. The sight of it still brought a lump to his throat. He watched the young riders leave the arena in a wild race after the grand entry of the rodeo, searching for Elena among the group. He spotted her, so proud and beautiful in her new clothes. The queen contest was held earlier before the show officially began. The winner would be announced after today's performance. He hoped Elena did well in the barrel race and the pole bending. She roped calves and the goats well enough in a corral, but the roping here was a lot different, and faster. On the ranches, accuracy was what counted. No one wanted their stock run, as it stressed the animal and made them lose weight.

Elena was leaning against their old stock trailer after hauling a bucket of water to her horse. They both were tired, but had done very well. Elena had even placed in the breakaway roping. The cheering of Carol and her friends every time she entered the arena was almost embarrassing, but nice too. In a few minutes they would announce the all-around winners and the queen. Manuel came limping up.

"You better get back on your horse to accept the prizes," he said. He patted Elena's arm as he untied the horse and gave her the reins. He was so proud of her, he didn't know what to say.

The riders all lined up at the gate, hoping to hear their names called for an award. Elena was called for each event she had entered. The applause was wild by the time she was announced girls' all-around champion. It seemed the whole truck stop was in the stands applauding and whistling. The announcer cleared his throat for the final award, the girls' queen contest.

"This year's contest was a tough one for the judges. Their decision is final, however, and the winner is Elena Sanchez!"

Elena heard Carol scream as a bouquet of roses was brought to her and, through her own tears, saw her father wipe a sleeve across his eyes as he stood leaning on the fence.

Carol was waiting at the trailer for Elena, camera in hand. She took Elena's picture to put up in the store after giving her a kiss and hard squeeze.

"Elena, whether you won or not, you are a winner. Remember that. And never forget that people love you and believe in you."

Manuel took the flowers and new shiny buckle from his daughter so she could load her horse. She hugged the horse's tired neck before sending him into the trailer.

"Papa, I will buy us a hamburger on the way out of town. I can afford that!" Elena's eyes twinkled at her father as she waved her check at him. Her long hours spent practicing had paid off, not just with the check, but with respect for her riding and her horse. She didn't tell her father she planned to put the rest toward pipe for the new well.

Elena got out of the truck to open the wire gate for her father to drive through. She saw tracks in the dust leading to their place, and pointed them out to Manuel.

Manuel hung his head out of the window to study the tire tracks as he drove through. Elena climbed back in after closing the gate and asked her father who he thought it was that had come in their absence.

"I don't know. Maybe we will find something out when we get to the house."

The pickup crawled down the rise to the homestead of old trailers. Elena got out and began unloading her horse. She was tired and was trying to decide if she had the energy left to haul and heat the water necessary for a bath. She finally noticed Manuel had not moved, but was staring at something.

"What are you doing, Papa?"

As Elena came up with her horse she saw tears on her father's weathered cheek for the second time that day.

"What is the matter, Papa? Que paso?" Elena was alarmed, and frightened to see her father this way, not moving or saying a word.

Elena followed her father's stare to a roll of black pipe left near the pens.

Manuel cleared his throat.

"Nothing. Nothing is wrong." His voice broke with emotion.

"We are blessed, Elena. God has sent us help. He has sent angels to help you with the rodeo, to find work for us, to help us buy this place and find our water. Now, he has sent more to bring this pipe. We will have running water to our house, even to the pens! Read the note."

Elena finally saw the crumpled paper in her father's hand. She took it from his clenched fist and smoothed it out. It simply said, "Good luck and God bless!"

Manuel reached for his daughter and held her tight. At long last they had found a home. One with angels.

WINDY RIDGE

I wrote this when my college-aged son was diagnosed with a rare
disease that causes tumors to form in the brain and spine. It was a
devastating blow, something that I could not accept for a long time.
I've always sought a horse and a lonely place in times of deep trouble.

Up on Windy Ridge I see the Guadalupes rise
And watch an eagle soar and glide through azure skies.
I see the Cornudas across the grasslands below
The Organs' pillars of gray barren rock a dull glow.

The horse and I have journeyed here alone
More alienated than I have ever known.
Seeking answers that refuse to be found
We struggle to climb to the highest ground.

Artifacts lay in the dust of this peak
Remnants of past peoples who came to seek
Visions and direction to lead their way
While I simply kneel and reverently pray.

I do not expect a voice or vision
Seeking guidance and profound decision
But I open my soul and plead my case
In what I believe is a Holy place.

I rise and try to store the view I savor
Wondering if I have somehow found favor
Before I begin the rough ride to descend
And leave my prayers floating on the wind.

THE MUSTANGER

The old dented pickup truck bounced across the alkaline desert, its outdated stock racks rattling on the bed, followed by a plume of grayish white dust the consistency of ash. The dust had become a part of the three men long ago, settling on everything God or man had made in the high desert valley.

The driver squinted, deepening the lines in his weathered face and pointed with one crooked finger directly ahead at the water tank in the hazy distance.

"Keep a look out for him, boys."

His two sons peered through the dirty windshield. Though neither had hit twenty-five, their faces already bore the lines and patina of the high desert.

The wind began to blow, rolling the baby-powder fine dust up over the sage while a dust devil formed and spun in front of them.

Guy wheeled the pickup around a large greasewood plant and stopped. Father and sons watched the bay stud cautiously approaching the water hole. The mares and colts of the stud's band now appeared from behind a low hill near the spring. The mares were playing the role of scouts, ensuring the way was safe. The stud had watched his band intently and tested the air with flared nostrils before coming in to drink.

These feral horses had helped him pay for this place. Without them, the family could never have held on during the bad years of drought, low cattle prices, or too much snow. The horses made good ranch horses when the ranchers were still allowed to manage them. The old practice of culling studs too long in the gene pool and replacing them with a well-bred horse had helped the herds. The horses had fewer birth defects, were more intelligent and attractive, and brought better prices. The cull horses they captured were sold for dog food. These horses were not mustangs, had never had Spanish lineage. They were descendants of horses turned out to make their own living after the World Wars, when the market crashed. Guy still lived by the old code, before the laws made doing anything beyond watching them a federal offense.

"Let's sit tight a minute. Make sure no one's around, boys," Guy finally said.

Trey studied the area through binoculars, looking for the telltale plume of dust a vehicle would make. Nothing moved out here without stirring up the alkali powder.

"Nothing. I don't see nothing but some cows starting in for water, way off."

Guy climbed out of the truck, grabbing a rope he began to shake out.

"You boys stay in the truck. I'll rope him out of the bed."

Guy's sons' eyes met and locked, their expressions carefully hidden.

"Dad, let's go get the horses. We got time," pleaded Troy, motioning behind him where the tin roofs of the ranch buildings dully shone across the valley.

The use of horses would ensure better control of the animal more quickly, with less risk to the horse or men. Despite the wind blowing the dust, a pickup would kick up enough dust to be seen from the highway. Guy stared his sons down.

"Trey, you drive. Troy, you get the other ropes ready," Guy instructed as he climbed into the truck bed.

"Dad, it's gonna be next to impossible to even get a shot at him with those racks on," Trey halfheartedly argued.

"Just get in there and drive. I'll show you what I can do. You put me where I need to be, and we'll have him slicker than snot."

Guy's sons shook their heads and climbed back into the truck.

"Let's go." Guy's tone cut through any impending argument. "Get me up there so I can get a decent shot! The wind is blowing and the dust will cover us."

Trey started the truck. His father hung on to the racks as the truck bumped over chamisa and low sage on its way toward the band of horses. Guy whistled at the stud to catch the horse's attention, then made a guttural, blowing sound as the truck neared. The stud threw his head up, and danced a few feet. Guy blew again, the stud stomping and holding his ground.

"Go, go now!" Guy yelled to Trey.

The truck swung in parallel to the horse, closing the distance rapidly.

Trey tried to keep his father in view while circling ever closer to the bay horse. He heard his father yell again and mashed the gas, tailspinning the truck sideways toward the horse. A loop shot through the air.

Trey slowed the pickup to a stop as muffled shouts sounded.

"What did he say?" asked Trey as he began backing up.

"He said for you to stop!" answered Troy, anxiously scanning the mirror on his side of the truck.

Trey stopped the truck as a loud thud sounded.

"What was that? Was that him banging on the truck for us to stop?" he asked his brother.

"Hell, I don't know!" Troy exclaimed as he stuck his head out the window.

"I still can't see shit. He'll probably be pissed, but I'm getting out to see what's going on," Troy said as he threw open the passenger door.

Troy stepped out into a greasewood, the thorns adding to his aggravation, and yelled at his brother. "I don't see him!"

"Crazy old man. What did he do, let that 'stang drag him off the truck?" Trey swore as he joined Troy to scan the area.

"There's the damn horse, right over there. And I don't see no rope or the old man," Trey said, scanning the area.

The low moan was barely audible.

"Dad? Dad, where are you?" Trey called as he quickly turned in a circle, surveying the area.

"Good God! He's under the truck!" hollered Troy, following the churned-up ground leading under the pickup.

Both men dived under the truck to find their father white-faced, blood frothing out of his mouth.

Guy tried to speak and coughed one last time.

"Dad, damn it! Dad, don't do this!" Trey rose up, grabbed his father's shirt and banged his head on the truck's driveline.

Troy wiggled over, buried his face in his father's dust-coated jacket, and sobbed, "He's gone, ain't he? Oh, God!"

Trey looked at his younger brother and felt a tightness around his heart that seemed to paralyze his breathing. He pulled his brother's arms away from their father.

"Come on, Troy. Let's get out from under here. Come on, now," he coaxed.

Trey felt suddenly old as reality began crashing down on him. What were they going to do now? Being the oldest, he felt the full, sickening weight of responsibility. He had always tried to look out for his little brother.

"Troy, we gotta figure this out. I know it is hard to think right now, but we got to. Get ahold of yourself."

Trey put his arm around his brother's shaking shoulders. He bent down and grabbed Troy's hat, beat it against his leg to knock the dust off, and handed it to his ashen-faced brother. He cleared his throat, and took a deep breath.

"We have a real situation here," he said. "Now, don't look at me that way."

"How in the hell can you just stand there, with Dad lying there under that truck? We killed him! You and me, his own sons, killed him!" sobbed Troy.

"Now, you shut up! You know this was an accident. Get ahold of yourself. Things are gonna get a whole lot worse if we don't do something real quick. This was sure enough an accident, but what about chasing the mustangs? Do you think Dad would want us in prison?" Trey demanded.

"All right then," Trey continued. "Dad worked hard all his life so we boys would have this place. In case you have forgotten, we were committing a felony when this whole thing went wrong. What do you think a jury would think? I can see it all now. For them, it is only a small step from mustanging to manslaughter."

Troy stood hunched over, drawing a line in the dust with his boot. He looked up at his brother, tears still making pathways on his dusty face.

"Go on, I'm listening," he managed to croak out.

"Way I see it, we only got one choice. Take Dad on home. Run some cows in the corral. We'll say he was run over in the corral."

"Oh, God, Trey. You mean take Dad and lay him in the corral

and run cows over him?"

"If you have a better idea, let me in. I sure don't intend on spending any time behind bars, and you know Dad would tell us to do what we had to."

The brothers carefully pulled their father out from under the truck. Trey bent over his father and tenderly wiped the blood-caked dust from his face.

"Dad, damn you, anyway. Why wouldn't you listen? Now look at what we have to do," he sobbed.

Straightening up, he looked at his brother. "Come over here and give me a hand. We're going to have put him in the truck. That way if we run into anyone, they can say they saw him here with us."

"You mean sit him up, with us?" asked Troy, horrified.

"Like I said before, you got any better ideas, I am all ears, brother."

They placed Guy in the center of the seat, hands in his lap and hat pulled down low for the last ride in the old truck. Trey walked back around the truck and grabbed a cedar limb to wipe out the tracks, praying the wind stayed up to drift over the scene.

The truck bounced and rattled over the desert, causing Guy to begin sliding forward. Troy stared out the window, refusing to believe what was happening or acknowledge that his arm was now around his dead father's shoulder. The reality was too much to absorb.

They pulled into the ranch yard without meeting a single soul. Trey drove behind the outbuildings and looked out at the meadow where the cows they'd gathered and brought home yesterday grazed. The men laid their father down on the truck seat, covering him with an old blanket.

"Don't worry about him none. He'd be the first to tell us what we're doing is right. You know that, Troy," Trey stated flatly.

"Let's just get this over with," was all Troy could manage to say as he followed Trey to the barn for their horses. He'd never realized how much his brother was like his father.

Dust hung thick over the corrals when the sheriff and coroner arrived an hour and a half later. Guy's sons were standing guard over their prostrate father, while cattle milled around the corral. Two horses stood tied to the fence, heads hung low, dried sweat streaking their flanks. The nervous cattle stopped and stared at the men through the fine haze of dust. The coroner followed the sheriff closely, leery of the wide-eyed cattle.

"What happened, boys?" asked the sheriff, motioning the boys to join him while the coroner bent over Guy's lifeless body. "When you called, the dispatcher said there had been an accident."

Trey spoke first. "We was working these cows, Troy and me a'horseback. Dad was working the gate on foot. We couldn't hardly see what happened for all the dust, but I guess some of the cows we cut out and headed for the gate run over Dad. We didn't even know anything was wrong 'til he didn't answer us when we hollered at him."

"So, you say a cow run over him? Where? Which gate was he working?"

Mustang Spring

"That gate there, sir. And it probably wasn't just one cow," Troy responded without lifting his head. "Trey had cut some out, and so had I. We figure both groups probably hit there 'bout the same time."

"Son, look at me. There's no need to be ashamed of crying," the sympathetic sheriff said softly, studying Troy's face.

The sheriff waved the cattle out of his way as he walked over to the coroner.

"What's it look like, Bud?" he asked the man bent over Guy's dusty, lifeless body. Hoof prints and the filth of the corral plainly showed. "Do we need to have an autopsy?"

Bud, the coroner, pushed his glasses back up on his nose as he straightened up. "What do they say happened, and then I'll tell you," he replied.

"They say he was run over in that gate by some cows. They couldn't see exactly what happened because of the dust."

"Let's go talk to them," Bud said, picking up his bag.

The sheriff cleared a path for the coroner through the milling cows.

"I'm watching these cows," the sheriff said. "They sure are nervous. They probably only see these corrals once a year. This is big country down here. Probably lucky to do that."

The coroner agreed.

"I don't believe I'll turn my back to them," he said.

Troy and Trey watched the men approaching them.

"Just be cool. It's almost over," Trey told his brother in a low voice.

The coroner asked the brothers a few questions before turning to the sheriff.

"I don't think we need an autopsy," he said. "The boys have already been through enough, and I won't find anything that isn't obvious." He didn't add he was shorthanded and behind in his work at his office, fifty miles away.

"Thank you, sir," Trey answered. "My brother and I have been through plenty today. Law still says we can bury him ourselves if we do it in twenty-four hours, doesn't it?"

The sheriff answered, "It does. Figuring on burying your dad here on the place? Bud and I will just step over here and finish our reports."

"Yes, sir. He always said that's what he wanted," Trey said. "Over on that hill yonder, where he could watch everything."

The sheriff looked to where Trey pointed.

"He'll have quite a view there," he said. "See the ranch and everything in this end of the valley. Look, there's some mustangs up there now."

Troy followed the sheriff's gaze to see the bay stud and his band crossing the hill. He swore the stud looked down at the men and reared before following his mares in the last light of the day.

DEATH AT CORNUDAS

I was reading Jack Thorpe's book, Pardner in the Wind, about his time spent in New Mexico, when it occurred to me that the story I was reading took place in an area of the ranch where a daughter and son-in-law were working, about fifty miles south of our ranch. As I read further, I discovered the ranch they lived on was part of this story, a story no one had ever put to song or verse. I decided it should be shared, and I tried to stay as true as I possibly could to Jack's narrative. The grave is still visible, as is what's left of the dugout home. I also used the town of Carlsbad's original name of Eddy.

Sick and abandoned, down off Crow Flats
She and two boys to live like rats.
The worthless man left her there to fend
Knowing in his heart she wouldn't mend
That, lungers coughing and spitting blood
Shouldn't live in shacks of rock and mud.
Three walls of malapais loosely stacked
One dismal room on the Butterfield track.
They dug and scratched a dreary living
On land better at taking than giving.
Neighbors wouldn't let a family starve
Sometimes left a haunch to carve
When they gathered and trailed stock
To the spring tank in the rock.

The older boy came riding to Bill's
On a bony horse to Windy Hill.
"Mr. Bill, Ma's died," he finally said
Squeezing tears back for his dead
While the younger sat with his ma
Lifeless on a sorry bed of straw.
Bill, John and I were simple cowpokes
But did our best for these folks.
Barren range of rock and little wood
John tore down his chicken house where it stood
Dug in the rock by Cornudas Tanks

121

Deanna Dickinson McCall

Buried her, coffin made of the planks
Carefully lined with his clean white shirts
Tacked down to keep out the drifting dirt.

We said a few words over the grave
While the little boys tried to be brave
Made a cross from the busted shovel
To mark the spot near the sad hovel.
The Joe Ray family was now broken.
Not a word of "father" was spoken.
Bill took the orphaned boys to his place
Gathered their livestock and found a space
In Eddy for the boys and a school.
The old bachelor was nobody's fool.
Let the cattle and horses increase
Never took out money for care or lease.
The boys would have a stake one day
Due to Mr. Bill's generous way.

It is quiet as death here today.
Even the wind is staying away.
There's little left to show they were here.
Tell the sad saga of yesteryear.
The forlorn grave is just a rock mound
Raised up slightly from the rocky ground.
The boys grew up and moved far away
No kin ever laid claim to Ms. Ray.

Stories by the ancients are pecked high
In shadow of the relentless sky
Above the sacred Cornudas Tank
Where they once danced and drank.
Symbols chiseled by lean brown fingers
Their fierce presence still lingers
Watching over the woman alone
Buried beneath the unmarked stone.

THE PERFECT FATHER

Sunbeams slanted through the dirty window, forming a halo-like haze around the baby sitting on the kitchen floor and surrounded with dented pots and lids. Sara clanged the pot lids together again, smiling at her chubby fists as Becky jumped. Biting her already ragged bottom lip, she sighed and continued stirring the pot on the stove, glancing at the dusty old clock. Like everything else in the house, it needed cleaning. As she stepped toward the refrigerator, her heavy winter boots tried to stick to the linoleum. It was fall, a busy time on the ranch. With her husband gone so often, the majority of the ranch work fell on her young shoulders, leaving little time for housework.

She picked the baby up and placed her in the highchair. She tried to summon a smile at her daughter as she fed her, gently wiping Sara's tender skin. Becky managed to eat a few bites of her own fragrant stew, though she felt no hunger, only a gnawing that seemed constant lately. She glanced once more at the clock, then gathered up the few dishes they had dirtied and placed them on the pile near the sink.

He wasn't coming for lunch. He wouldn't come back until tonight, if then.

Becky turned her gray eyes toward the heap of winter clothes dropped at the door. She dressed her daughter in layers of warm, soft clothing and blankets before she pulled on her own coat, hat and gloves. It was miserably cold. She'd just have to leave the truck running. Sara would sleep in her car seat and never miss her mother.

After loading the baby and the diaper bag, she allowed the two ranch dogs to join her. She drove a few miles down the dirt road to the shipping pens. They were deserted now, save for a few head of cows. Her eyes followed her husband's pickup tracks, mingled with the buyer's and the cattle truck's in the light skiff of snow. They were headed to town and the nearest bar.

She set the parking brake and eased quietly out of the truck, checking that Sara was still asleep. The big engine ran smoothly, the heater surrounding the baby with warmth. The dogs joined her, leaping and crouching in turn, excited at the prospect of cattle still remaining. Scattering hay outside the corrals, Becky felt the cold stinging her face. Her already stiffened hands fumbled with the latch on the gate.

The hungry cattle poured out, pushing and shoving to get at the hay. Anger began to replace the sadness she felt. Her father would have never treated stock this way. What had Mike planned to do, leave them without feed until he remembered to come home? She silently scolded herself for making the comparison between the two men, something she found she was doing a lot lately.

She had helped load the trucks this morning and heard the buyer say it would be a couple of days before he sent another truck out for the cull cows. Becky wished she had stayed at the pens, at least long enough to get the check, instead of going home to fix lunch, as Mike asked. Hopefully the bank was closed before he made it into town.

The sun was lowering itself to the cold blue mountains behind her. Becky tried to stomp some feeling back into her frozen feet, then climbed into the warm truck, where Sara was still sleeping, the dogs joining her. She rested her forehead against the steering wheel wearily.

As she pulled into the ranch, she spotted cattle in the pens adjoining the barn. She'd have to add them to the chore list. Cuddling Sara against herself, she grabbed the diaper bag and made her way into the house. She added wood to the coals left in the stove and placed the sleeping baby gently in the playpen before heading out for evening chores.

Lavender twilight had descended upon the ranch. After forking hay to the hospital pen of cattle and then the horses, she climbed up to the top rail to look over the animals. Their breath showed as puffs of steam, as did hers. Stars began appearing in a sky gone inky dark. "Oh, Daddy," she pleaded softly to the blackened sky.

Becky sighed raggedly as she lowered her troubled face and stared across the corrals. She loved this ranch and way of life. It was her legacy, and Sara's. Becky's father, Joe, and her grandfather had put years of sweat and blood into the ranch. Joe had taught her everything she knew. To Joe and his daughter the ranch was always their priority. Now, the man Becky had married was falling short, and the reality was brought home as a single tear slid down her dirty face. Becky pushed herself off the fence and wiped the show of weakness away.

She slowly shook her delicate head to clear thoughts of Mike as she strode back to the barn. Before she entered the house, the frigid air had turned into a glittering mist.

Becky gave a smile to her daughter playing in her playpen. Thank God for whoever invented the playpen, Becky thought. She washed her chapped hands, then began pulling out food and pans. She set Mike's place, carefully lining up the silver on the napkin, though she never looked at it again during the meal.

The quiet evening wore on and Becky's thoughts drifted again to her father. She lay her head back against the couch and closed her eyes. She missed him so much, especially on nights like this. He had raised her alone, ever since the tragic accident that left her mother dead and Joe scarred. Becky knew the scars inside him were twisted and ugly, more terrible even than the disfigurement that showed. He had always refused to speak of the wreck. She had heard someone say Joe was never the same man after that night, that Joe blamed himself for his wife's death. In Becky's adoring eyes, he had done a wonderful job filling the role of both parents.

Mustang Spring

She couldn't remember Joe ever leaving an animal hungry or uncared for. And he would never leave Becky alone so much, like Mike did. She knew the remoteness of the ranch was hard for her fun-loving husband to adjust to, but she had also discovered it wasn't only people he missed. It seemed the drinks in the bar filled a void in him but, in Becky's eyes, his insecurities and loneliness were no excuses for shirking responsibilities.

When Becky woke alone the next morning, the windows were coated with ice in beautiful patterns reminiscent of swirled flowers. She remembered her mother guiding her tiny finger over the ice flowers, telling her they were made by the ice fairies. Trying to escape things that were no more and would never be again, she jumped out of bed. Hurrying to keep warm, she opened the stove, watching as pine splinters sparked and caught as she added them to the glowing embers. She picked Sara up, holding her tightly against her breast as if savoring the warmth of another human. Becky didn't realize how lonely she was at times.

Deciding to stall a while and let the slowly rising sun warm things up, she walked over to the old rolltop desk and pulled out the ranch ledger. After a careful hour of figuring and including the sale they made yesterday, they could just pay their bills. If Mike hadn't spent or lost it. The payment for the mortgage they'd had to put on the ranch to buy more cows loomed ahead, as did countless other expenses.

Becky cleared a place in a window wet with melting ice to look at the thermometer nailed to the post of the front porch. It was late enough now that chores had to be done, regardless of the cold. Cattle had to be fed, ice broken, and stock checked. Daylight hours were short in the deep of winter. Becky took a deep breath before she began bundling up Sara and herself.

By that evening, she was worn out, fatigued from lifting hay bales that nearly matched her weight and the ever-deepening cold that seemed to settle in her bones. After a supper of warmed-up leftovers, she and Sara soaked in a hot bath until the water lost its comforting warmth and became gray and lukewarm. Becky settled in the flannel sheets and heavy quilts and fell into a deep sleep, too exhausted to dream of the past or the future.

The next morning, while the air still smelled of the heavy sweetness of pancake syrup and she stood scrubbing the last of the crusted dishes, Becky remembered the cattle buyer was supposed to send the last truck today. Sara was cooing and trying to clap her chubby hands as she watched her young mother worriedly take her bottom lip once again between her small square teeth while coming to the decision she would have to go to the shipping pens first to feed. She'd released the cattle to graze a couple days ago. Now she'd have to run them back in, and she'd better take a horse in case the lure of hay wasn't sufficient.

With a horse in tow, and nearing the pens, she wondered if she should have tried to call Mike. The problem was, where? She figured he was probably sleeping it off in the back room of a bar. Her pride wouldn't allow her to be the butt of jokes about her calling and looking for her wayward husband.

Becky gave Sara a bottle, smiling gratefully at her good-natured baby. The baby was wrapped in layers of blankets, tied up like a minute bedroll in the car seat. Becky carefully closed the pickup door. She went to the back of the trailer and unlatched the door before climbing in to untie the horse and lead him out. The old manure in the trailer was frozen and the horse slid on the brown-colored ice while backing up. Becky blew her warm breath into her heavy gloves before quickly pulling them back on after tightening the cinch, the few moments of her skin being exposed already painful. She tied the patient horse to the trailer and stepped around to begin calling the cattle. The call had been in her family for generations, and it sounded through the frigid air, carrying a hint of the Highlands.

Some of the cattle began to drift toward the corral, answering her call, as she spread hay. A few were too far out to hear her call or see the hay. Checking on Sara, safe inside the pickup sleeping soundly, she mounted Hank. He was an older, seasoned horse who Becky relied on when she was forced into chores and circumstances like this.

Carefully picking their way over the frozen ground, Becky's toes barely in the stirrups, the two circled wide around the oblivious cows, heading them toward the hay-strewn corral. She rode in after the last cow and eased Hank over to swing the gate closed, just as a brocklefaced cow started for the gate. With Becky still leaning over to the side to free the stuck gate, Hank whirled to face the cow, his feet slipping on the icy ground as he scrambled in vain to regain his balance. Becky tried to pull herself clear of the falling horse by grabbing for the gate, but Hank's body fell, pinning her between the gate and the horse's body. She felt every bar smack her as she was mashed against the gate, finally coming to rest pinned to the unyielding frozen ground. Hank scrambled up, shaking himself and looking toward the cow. Becky lay still, pain radiating into a thick haze. Slowly a picture of Sara in the truck broke through the fog in her mind.

Stay calm, she repeated dumbly to herself. It will be all right. She tried to rise, pulling on the saddle of the patient horse still guarding the gate. A scream of agony filled her ears, sending Hank whirling away from her. Becky heard the scream, which seemed to come from far way, from another place and from someone else, and panicked at the raw animalistic sound. Oh God, help me, she prayed, collapsing on the frozen ground.

Fighting waves of nausea, Becky tried to shake her head. She knew the danger she and Sara were facing. She tried to crawl toward the truck, tears freezing on her agonized face. It was the last thing she remembered.

Becky woke groggily in an unfamiliar white room, her body throbbing and pulsating with aching. Raising her head made sweat bead on her bruised face while her neck corded with the effort. She tried to call out Sara's name again and again, gagging on the painful dryness of her throat.

Mike's voice tried to reach her through the haze and fog, telling her over and over again to lie still, and how sorry he was. The smell of stale whiskey, barroom smoke and old sweat was floating around her. She tried to focus her swollen eyes and saw her husband standing over her.

Mike was unwashed, unshaven, and looked like he had aged ten years. He spoke quietly, his voice breaking when he told her the truck driver had found her and called for an emergency helicopter. Sara had been safe in the pickup, with Hank still guarding Becky and the gate. Mike tried to smile through tears that filled his bloodshot eyes as he added the last bit about Hank. Upon hearing Sara was safe, Becky closed her weary eyes, and tried to drift back to the quiet place she had found.

Vague images and sounds began to appear — flashing lights, masked faces with sharp eyes reporting broken ribs, pelvic fractures, and a concussion. Exhausted from trying to remember, she fell asleep.

The next morning, Mike sat beside her bed, showered and as handsome as ever. The fresh scent of his cologne came to Becky before she opened her eyes. He took her small, roughened hand in his large hand, carefully avoiding her purple and yellow bruises. She turned her head away to hide the painful wince as she tried to pull her swollen hand free from his grasp.

"Becky, damn it, listen to me. I can never forgive myself for what happened. Now I know what your dad went through. He didn't get a second chance. My drinking days are over."

Mike's voice broke when he added, "Becky, I love you so much."

Becky searched his face, noting the green eyes swimming with tears, threatening to spill over his freshly shaven cheeks. The room was silent except for the machines monitoring Becky. Finally, she asked in a low voice "What do you mean about Dad?"

"Why, the guilt he felt for making you grow up without your mother. He quit too late to save your mother, but he stayed on the wagon to raise you. Didn't you ever wonder why he avoided town? He couldn't stand facing folks who knew what happened."

Becky struggled to sit up, shouting, "Are you saying he killed my mother because he was drunk? Don't you dare try to make up stories to cover your own problems!"

A nurse ran in, ordering Mike out of the room, and adding a sedative to Becky's IV line. The medication began to take effect, and Becky closed her eyes. Dreamlike voices from her childhood came, bits of conversation, and vaguely familiar faces appeared.

"We tried to take his keys. He wouldn't listen."

"He ended up killing her, instead of himself, with his drinking."

"Poor child. Joe killed her mother."

Mustang Spring

When Becky woke that afternoon, she painfully remembered her dreams. Slowly things began to fall into place. Her father's lack of interest in anything in town, or their neighbors. Her home schooling, then boarding school in another state. No alcohol was ever permitted in the house, not even the customary bottle for emergencies.

She was staring at the wall, deep in thought, when Mike appeared, with Sara in his arms. Sara reached her chubby arms out for her mother, and Mike gently laid the baby next to Becky. The idea of how close she came to never seeing her daughter again brought fresh tears and a deeper ache to Becky's chest. With a ragged breath, she closed her eyes and thanked God.

A nurse appeared, telling Mike he had five more minutes left to visit. He cleared his throat of the lump that had formed and looked Becky straight in the eye.

"I thought you knew about the wreck and your dad, or I would never have upset you like that," he said. "I thought you knew he was an alcoholic and that was why you hated me drinking so much. Joe was a good man, Becky, but not perfect. I'm not perfect either, but I plan to change things, to be there for you and Sara. I went to an AA meeting last night and learned a few things. That I am human, and I have insecurities. That I have to deal with those insecurities. I'll still be going to town, but it will be for the meetings. No matter what happens, Becky, I want to be there for you."

Mike gently reached for her hand, and Becky felt a sense of sadness settle over her. She wanted Sara to grow up with both parents, and she still loved Mike. But she couldn't trust him.

Becky cleared her throat.

"Mike, I still love you. I realize I probably added to your insecurities by unfairly comparing you to my dad. But, you are still responsible for your actions. I don't need a baby to raise, a man acting like a teenager, and a ranch to run. If you want to try to make this work, it will be on my terms. My bones will heal, but my heart may never knit. I won't make promises I can't keep."

As Mike bent over to kiss his wife, tears of quiet gratitude for a second chance fell on her face. He prayed he could be as strong as his wife.

OLD CORRALS

These older corrals are in sad disrepair and lay a short distance, around the river's bend, from our headquarters. Juniper trees, cholla and algarita grow in them now. They raised the question of why there are two sets of corrals so close together. An old-timer told me an argument took place there, with two men who shared the corrals throwing rocks at each other. Someone made a monument of two piles of rocks to represent both sides.

How many cattle? How many years?
How many men? Who were the pioneers
That chose this place to gather stock?
To pen his herd or flock?

Who chose where the mountains bend and curve
Widening into a flat that would serve…
Where an ancient cottonwood stands guard
Of the river's entry to the ranch yard?

When was the first post driven in this ground?
Did the canyon echo with the sound?
Picket posts handhewn and wire laced
Pole gates with crude hardware placed.

How many light-footed horses danced
Pirouetting and proud as they pranced
Tossing heads with shiny manes, nostrils wide
At cattle with long horns and spotted hides?

How many cattle churned this soil
While ropes snaked out from their coil?
Were cinch rings used when they felt the need
Or did honor override their greed?

The old concho I clutch is a keepsake
Found this morning after daybreak
Under a cinch ring broken and black
Seeking a spotted cow's track
Riding a horse with light dancing feet
Where the old corrals and mountains meet.

Mustang Spring

THE HIRED HAND

This is a true story, and actually did happen to me, much to my chagrin!

We made a call to town
To have some help sent down.
The horses and us were wore out.
I even walked like I had gout.

They said they'd send a gal out.
She knew what riding was about.
We agreed it would be all right
And she'd arrive that night.

After supper I heard a truck come in
And went to check the bunkhouse again.
I was surprised to find her there.
It did kinda give me a scare.

Well, she was experienced all right
And I was grateful for the poor light.
She looked so old and poor
Standing slumped in that door.

141

Deanna Dickinson McCall

Her battered hat had a hole in the crown
And strands of dirty hair hung down
Over a face lined with dust and crud
That water would have turned to mud.

There was a tattered scarf round her neck.
Her coat looked like she'd been in a wreck.
One sleeve was tore halfway loose
Where feathers floated in search of the goose.

Just as I was about to voice my doubt
I let out a strangled shout.
Recognition had come to me
And I tried to gather some dignity.

For all my fears had come true
And there wasn't a thing I could do
But slam that bunkhouse door
And not look in that damn mirror any more!

AN EDUCATION

The classroom was old and warm, with the stale smell of chalk and floor wax. The freshman in the back of the class felt sweat bead on his lip and found it increasingly difficult to sit still. He wished he could open a window and let in some of the fresh, freezing air.

Times like this were when he really missed the freedom of the ranch. The American history teacher standing at the front of the class called herself an environmentalist and was proudly telling about her latest endeavor, some sort of a "save the coyote" campaign. Last month it was about sagebrush becoming endangered. He'd laughed aloud and was given detention.

She blamed everything on people from the West, beginning with the first pioneers who cut trees and killed predators that endangered their livelihood. It was amazing she found no fault with the Pilgrims or all the folks who destroyed all the forests to build New York City.

As she went on extolling the virtues of the coyote, memories from last spring flashed before the boy. The new calf he and his dad had put in the barn when the mother cow died during the difficult birth. Two hours later, the calf was dead with a gaping hole at its still-warm flank and three young coyote pups were spotted running out of the adjoining corrals. Or when they were glassing the meadows in search of cows having problems and spotted the pack, surrounding a cow they'd run out on the ice, jumping and snapping to pull out the half-emerged calf while the cow tried desperately to stand on the ice field and fight.

Billy felt hotter yet as anger grew. He raised his hand to speak and his effort was ignored. Probably for the best, he thought. He'd end up in the principal's office if he said what he really had on his mind. He'd be in even more trouble at home, if his folks heard of it. He wasn't raised to argue with his elders.

When the lunch bell rang, he hurried outside and waited for his friends. He and some of the other boys boarded in town to attend high school. The handful of boys dressed in jeans and shirts that actually fit them jumped into an old double-cab pickup to go eat. The school parking lot held few pickups. Ten years ago, most of the vehicles were ranch trucks. The ranch boys had become a minority in a world of baggy clothes, tattoos and body piercings.

Returning from lunch, the boys grabbed ropes out of the truck

146

and practiced their skills while rap music boomed from cars around them. Billy slowly recoiled his rope while wondering how his older friends stood it — the teachers, town, all of it. Some of the teachers were okay and understood, but others didn't have a clue, he thought. Some had the idea that living on a ranch was like an old romantic Western movie. Worse, some believed ranchers were "raping the earth" — that's what the civics teacher actually said. That teacher was also a vegan.

The rest of the day wore on until last period. This was the best part of school, range science class. At least in the Ag. room he could be comfortable, be himself. As he studied the slides showing grasslands with grazing and those without, an idea struck him. He asked permission to copy the photos and data. He'd present the materials to the history teacher, who believed all livestock should be removed from public lands. The teacher might not listen, but he could try.

After school, he got a ride to the stables. He was riding some colts for a couple of people. His folks thought it might help with homesickness if he could work with horses after school. Leading the first colt out, he stopped to scratch its neck and spoke softly to it. They had a lot in common. Both were ranch-raised and used to the freedom of open spaces.

"Guess you don't like being here any more than I do, do you, boy?" he asked. "They all think we need to see something besides the ranch. Think we need an education and to learn about the world. Guess we'd both run home fast as we could, given half a chance."

The colt slowly dropped his head to rest on the boy's shoulder, both of them staring out of town toward the mountains in the late afternoon sun.

At supper that night, he brought up the history teacher and her misguided views. His older friends knew how he felt, and told him they'd go rabbit hunting that evening after homework was done. It was a way for the boys to regain a little freedom during the week until they could go home to their families and ranches on Friday afternoons.

The truckload of boys and their .22- caliber rifles turned onto the dirt road ten feet past the city limit sign. They began bumping over the rough dirt road while the sun began to lower on the sagebrush plain. The boys leaned out their windows, letting the bracing air and freeze-dried dust flow freely over their youthful faces while they searched for their prey. The adjoining ranch raised sheep and alfalfa hay and the ranchers were glad the boys shot the rabbits that ate their crop.

"Something up ahead, right over the hill!" yelled Jesse, and the truck sped up, bouncing the slim, light boys nearly off the seat. The brakes slammed on and all the boys jumped out, ready to be the first to get a shot. A brownish blur moved through the brush and Cole shot, hollering, "Coyote!" The boys ran toward the commotion in the brush, to find the coyote in his last throes of life.

Cole picked up the coyote, and threw it in the back of the truck. "Dang, its getting cold!" he said as the boys clambered back into the truck. They shivered. The temperature had dropped as quickly as the sun. After driving a few more miles with no more success, they headed back toward town.

At the house, the boys put away their guns and got ready for bed.

"Hey, Billy, tomorrow's Friday," Jesse reminded him. "We get to go home." Billy was packing his bag. His mom would come into town in the late afternoon to get him and groceries. She couldn't come soon enough.

The next morning dawned breathtakingly cold, and the boys took turns scraping thick ice off the truck's windows. Billy threw his bag in the bed with the other boys' bags and jumped into the old truck, the defroster blowing loudly and doing little to warm up the boys. By the time they reached the school, a mile away, the vents had finally begun to produce lukewarm air.

The boys hurried into the school, looking forward to the warmth of the hallway. Billy got his books out of his locker and checked the folder he had made in his range science class the day before. He'd respectfully ask the history teacher to look at what he prepared, though he figured it was a useless effort. The ag teacher warned him she was beyond reaching. At least he could say he tried, he reassured himself.

Billy approached the history teacher a few minutes before class began. He politely asked her if she'd look over the data he'd prepared about the benefits to wildlife and the environment when grazing was practiced responsibly. She sneered and informed him his "ma'ms" didn't fool her, and she had better ways to spend her time than reading propaganda. She snatched the folder and tossed it into the trashcan beside her desk. He quietly sat through class, humiliated and angry.

At the morning break, Billy reflected that he'd rather be in the cold, like the coyote in the truck, when a thought struck him. Hurrying out, he slowed his pace and tried to appear casual as he went to the truck and peered into the back. The coyote had frozen solid, just as he'd expected.

He glanced around for the subcompact car with the sun shade across the windshield proclaiming EARTH FIRST!, and bumper stickers announcing the driver was a proud member of the Sierra Club, and a promoter of saving just about everything on earth but humans. Yep, she was here, parked across the street from the school. Hiding his smile, he decided his bag could stay put until after lunch.

Billy waited to make his move until lunch had ended and he and his buddies had re-entered the school. He announced he'd left his bag in the truck and ran back out. Making sure no one else was around, he crept across the road and tried the teacher's car door. It was unlocked.

He hurried back across the road and grabbed the coyote, now frozen into a semi-curled shape with its legs slightly curved inward. Glancing about to make sure he remained unseen, Billy knelt down and opened the driver-side door. He wedged the frozen coyote in the seat, placing the body upright behind the steering wheel so it appeared to be driving the car, the stiff front paws resting on the wheel.

Billy stepped back, stifling the mirth bubbling at the sight. He wished his buddies could see it, but didn't want them to get involved and get in trouble. He carefully closed the door and ran across the icy street to the truck. With a big smile, he grabbed his bag out of the back and ran inside the school. He wished he could be there when she opened the door. He wondered if she would call the cops. The weekend back at the ranch loomed ahead and Monday was a world away.

Mustang Spring

Deanna Dickinson McCall has cows, horses and a love of the land bred into her, coming from a family that began ranching in Texas in the 1840s. She has ranched in several western states, including twenty-five years spent raising her family on a remote Nevada ranch without phones or electricity. Riding on her own ranches, riding for day wages, receiving cattle at sale yards, and selling feed and vet supplies have given her fodder for her been-there, done-that stories and poetry. She and her husband and son ranch in the Sacramento Mountains of southern New Mexico.

CPSIA information can be obtained at www.ICGtesting.com
Printed in the USA
LVOW121402011112

305434LV00001B/17/P